FRIDAY BOYS

MICHAEL ARMSTRONG

JOHN O'RYAN

FRIDAY BOYS

Cocktail Cool, LLC
Wyoming, USA 2009

FRIDAY BOYS
by Michael Armstrong & John O'Ryan

Copyright © 2009 by Cocktail Cool, LLC
Cover design by Ryan McClure

P.O. Box 370
Hanna, WY
USA

ISBN-10: 0-9799994-6-4
ISBN-13: 978-0-9799994-6-8

www.cocktailcool.com

Dedicated to the loving memory of Leanne Spencer, a great friend and teacher to people all over the world.

CHAPTER 1

New York City
USA

Underneath John F. Kennedy Airport, the taxis and busses disperse weary travelers from every corner of the planet. The pick-up area is small and except for the glass of the terminal exit, resembles a well-used underground parking lot. The only lighting is from dim bulbs in the roof. It is night here all the time.

People often greet each other with hugs and handshakes in this travel limbo. Some will take the bus to Queens for eighteen dollars; others will cab it to Manhattan for the forty-dollar flat rate. It is here people inexperienced to the city first notice the fast paced talking and rushed walking of the native New Yorker.

Exiting the strip mall atmosphere of the terminal, a tall, muscular man carefully opened the doors pulling a trolley stacked with suitcases. He was careful not to jostle his more precious cargo; the bundled set of twins asleep in their chest harness. Side by side, they hung from his well-built pectorals like extensions of his chest. Their weight didn't seem to bother him as he maneuvered the trolley out of the steady stream of people.

After securing the trolley he adjusted the harness

slightly, satisfying himself the twin boy and girl were co-cooned properly in the shared papoose, blue half for him, pink for her. Looking up he saw a line of cabs stretching off to the left with a mix of drivers and customers mingling along the edge of the curb. Across the subterranean street a busy bus stop was crowded with people.

This is the place. Underground bus stop. There can't be too many of these.

He checked his watch and had a good look around the subterranean horizon. Satisfying himself his friend was not there yet, he sat down on the edge of his bag-laden trolley to wait.

I wonder how far Morrison, New Jersey is from here.

"Oh look at those little sugar bumpkins! Oh, they are so adorable!" Before he could look up, the woman was staring directly into his children's sleeping faces. She was captivated.

"They are…" He stood up so she didn't have to squat. As he rose she did as well, taking in his frame for the first time.

"Wow! You're a baby-transport machine." She erupted into nervous laughter, blushing a bit.

"We're attached at the hip, or should I say the chest." He caught her looking into his eyes and quickly looked down at the twins to focus her on them. "They've just hung there and done nothing all the way from Taiwan." He said, clutching their bottoms like they really were two huge hanging breasts.

"Taiwan?" She was laughing, and suddenly very interested.

6

Why did you have to tell her that? This is the fourth woman to ask about the twins since Taipei.

"Yeah. We just left Taiwan. For good." He smiled, surveying the area again. "We're waiting for a friend. We are Conrad, Peyton and I'm Cale." He extended his hand.

"And I'm Barbra. Barbra Spencer." She stared into his eyes as she shook his hand. She was over forty and still very beautiful. Her accent had New York all over it.

"That's funny, I have a friend named Barbra in Taiwan you remind me of."

"I'm gonna go now, Cale. Otherwise I might try and snatch you. Tall, gorgeous men, with beautiful twins growing out of their chest, tend to get snatched up around here. Tell your wife to be careful." Regaining a little of her New York composure, she flashed him a brilliant smile, twisted away, leaving just as suddenly as she'd appeared.

Cale checked his watch again.

How long has it been since their diapers were changed?

He turned, grabbing one of the bags next to him and opened it. Inside was an assortment of baby paraphernalia, including a softball-sized digital clock. Cale pushed the flat button on top and the clock spoke in a pleasant but hollow female voice.

"You have one hour until the next scheduled diaper check." He packed the clock back in the bag and closed it. Looking down at the sleeping faces, Cale found himself absorbed again. It had been like this the whole trip. Having the harness on made it overly easy to gaze at them. It was like staring into the flames of a hearty campfire; it soothed him and made him forget where he was. For the time being, that's exactly what Cale O' Rourke wanted. His mind started to drift, despite the squeal of car brakes and roar of buses echoing in the underground environment.

The eighteen-hour flight he had been dreading had gone off without a hitch. Cale had been on enough flights to know sometimes children on planes just cried. The twins had looked around, drooled a bit, eaten and then slept in unison. They had been brilliant, and despite his mistrust of the thin straps, so had the harness. He had even managed to sleep a little with them strapped to him, their tiny heartbeats undetectable, but their warmth and closeness calming in some primordial way. The airline had given him the seat next to him for the twins, but Cale had felt better with them strapped to his chest.

Sitting down, his body started to relax. He allowed it. Customs and the Department of Homeland Security had not been as daunting as Cale had thought they would be. Ever since he strapped his twins to his chest, everyone seemed to smile. When they learned that he was the father they rushed the paperwork. When they learned Cale was solo, the paperwork went even faster. Despite the complicated circumstances surrounding their nationality, his twin children seemed welcome everywhere, and him by proxy.

Cale watched a tall oriental woman step out of the terminal exit with a small leather duffle bag. She moved purposefully towards a bus marked E-3rd Street. It was leaving and she had to hurry.

Just as she reached the door, it closed. The woman banged savagely on the folding door of the bus, which was starting to move. The driver stopped and the door opened with a hydraulic hiss.

Cale smiled to himself and checked his watch again.

The woman getting on the bus reminded of another friend from Taiwan.

CHAPTER 2

Taichung City
Taiwan, R.O.C.

"I really like looking at your eyes," the smartly dressed Asian woman whispered in Cale's ear. He turned to face her.

Cale stared into her eyes while he kissed the pouting rouge lips. The female purred. A bell broke the kiss; they had come to her penthouse. The doors opened.

"I'm hungry. What have you got for me to eat this afternoon?" Cale asked, brushing bangs back from his face. She smiled at him. Together they walked out of the elevator hand in hand, as the doors shut.

In the apartment she walked straight to the bedroom. It was lavish with a lot of well-lit expensive space. She walked slowly to a table by the window. It was overcast but very bright and the room was flooded with a soft light. She was silhouetted against the window from where Cale stood at the door, watching. She put her clutch purse on the table.

"Cale, come here."

The words triggered a memory that haunted him often.

Grandview, Texas
(Ten Years Earlier)

"Cale, come here!" Jason Michael O'Rourke called from his bedroom. Cale peered in to the room where his mother and father slept. He didn't like the sound of his father's voice. It sounded how Cale imagined a lawyer would speak at the most serious part of a trial, even though his father was a banker. His financier father was angry.

"Cale, come here and sit down." Cale walked across the carpeted room with a lump in his throat and climbed into the rocking chair as his father continued to look out the window, doing up his tie. Cale always marveled at his father's ability to do it without a mirror.

"Your school called last night."

The lump in Cale's throat got bigger.

"I know you weren't there yesterday. Tell the truth, where were you?"

"At a friend's house." Cale began to tap his left foot, then stopped. Even at fifteen he knew this to be a culpable giveaway.

"Who was the friend?" Jason O'Rourke asked turning to face Cale while reaching for his suit jacket. Cale was staring at his treasonous foot.

"Caleb Ryan O'Rourke, I want an answer. Now!" His father stared at him with a suit jacket on, tie now folded into a tight knot. Jason Michael O'Rourke, Chief Financial Officer for Texas State Bank, was the unassailable authority-figure in fifteen-year-old Caleb O'Rourke's universe. His voice was angry.

"Dad, I don't know if you're gonna want to hear the truth."

"Cale, this is why we're talking. I do want to hear."

"Randy Warner."

"One of your classmates?"

"A friend."

"I assume his parents weren't home?"

"Randy's not a boy, Dad. And no, sir, her parents weren't home."

Jason took a deep breath. He let it out and asked, "What were you doing?"

"Stuff."

Randy really liked him. She had wanted to show Cale how much she liked him.

"Exactly what kind of 'stuff' were you two getting up to during a Tuesday afternoon when you should have been in school? You dropped off the grid for six hours young man. You took a major withdrawal from your 'trust' account with me. Now your mother is worried because she can't believe you did this and you missed your lessons. It wasn't drugs, I hope?"

"No, sir, it wasn't drugs."

Jason O'Rourke followed Cale's eyes to his left shoe. He was relieved a little. He now started thinking of other things Cale could have done.

"O.K. What was it?"

"I guess, probably, sex." Cale had no idea how his father was going to react.

"Define sex for me."

"Blowjob." Cale's voice was quieter.

Jason's mind went into overdrive. His son wasn't a

little boy any more, that wasn't news. He knew Cale was attracting girls with his good looks. The phone rang for the kid endlessly with some girl's voice on the other end. Point was, Jason had hoped the talks they had before would make him careful about having sex and when.

"O.K.... O.K. Oral sex."

"Yeah, oral sex." Cale's voice was even quieter.

"Just oral sex?"

"Just oral sex, Dad. No...nothing...nothing else. We didn't have a condom."

"No condom." Jason O'Rourke spoke softly as he said the words. He repeated one word in a question. "Condoms?"

Cale looked up at his dad, confused. *Why was his father having a hard time understanding this word?*

"O.K. This is a lecture, so listen up, my friend. We've had talks before about sex, but this one Cale O' Rourke, take heed." Jason looked to make sure he had his son's attention. He did. "I think I you need to respect the fact that sex has its time and place."

Cale nodded. His mind skipped back to the taste of lip-gloss. Her kiss was soft; her lips had tasted of the raspberry lip-gloss she always wore. The base of his penis had been coated in the stuff. Yesterday had definitely been an adventure. His father's voice brought him back to the present.

"Look, Cale, physically, you are almost a man, and I know you can have sex with or without my consent. I'm comforted you went no further because you had no condom. It's a good sign, in some ways." Jason cleared his throat. "What's wrong here is the fact you phoned the school and lied to them. The school, your mother and I entrust you to every day. That is inexcusable. Period, no debate." Jason cleared his throat one more time. "If there's one thing I want you to learn from me, one thing, it's that honesty – in all areas of life – is the key to becoming a good man. Tell the truth. Spineless people find excuses to lie."

"Dad, I couldn't tell the truth to the school."

"Then, Cale you shouldn't have been at your friend's place."

"Dad, didn't you ever do something like this?" Cale looked into Jason's eyes.

"Cale if I say, yes or no, it isn't the point. I'm telling you that if you want my respect, *mine*, you just have to be honest and truthful all the time. To achieve this you don't have to mark every word or weigh every action. Just don't allow yourself to be put in a position where you will have to lie. No matter what, it's that simple."

"No matter what?"

"No matter what. Liars have to remember every word they say. You just have to remember to think about your actions." Cale's father said revolving back to grab his cufflinks. He turned one last time to his son and said, "Really, Cale. No matter what. Promise me." Jason put his hand on Cale's shoulder. He gave the shoulder a strong squeeze and then patted it.

"O.K., Dad, I promise."

Jason O'Rourke removed his hand, turned and walked quickly across the carpet to the door. Cale sensed this would be the end of the matter. He breathed an internal sigh of relief. He had the coolest father.

The best.

Cale got up and looked at his watch. He had fifteen more minutes before his bus would take him to school. He contemplated about asking his dad for a ride, but thought better of it. His father had dropped the subject of the blow-job, and given him the pep talk. Promising to be honest forever was a small price to pay compared to how things could have gone down. No use in taking the chance of having yesterday's escapade coming up again in the car. Plus his mother would be there too and he didn't want to face her quite yet. The school bus seemed like a safer bet.

Three hours later, Cale was going over the molecular structure for citric acid in chemistry class when the loudspeaker in the room called him to the main office.

Great. Another lecture from a lesser authority.

He hoped his father would help a little in bailing him out. He usually helped defend Cale after he'd dropped the axe at home. In the meantime Cale would have to stand tall before Principal Saunders.

His teacher, Mr. Grayson, gave him a pass. The halls were empty. He went through the doors to the counter where his mother's good friend Norma Alne worked in administration.

Norma Alne was so close with his mother it was like having a second mom at school. She was on Cale's side most of the time, but like his parents, only after she'd had her say. Might as well let her get it over with now. She would give him that terse look over her glasses and point towards the principal's door. Cale didn't mind. She gave him a big friendly hug whenever he wasn't in trouble.

The door opened and Norma looked at Cale. She brushed away what looked like a tear. She took a deep breath. Her eyes were red and blotchy.

"Cale, you need to go in and see Principal Saunders." Norma's voice was quiet and strained. She looked very sad. It was Norma who had called to check up on Cale when she had heard he was ill. Cale remembered his mother saying something about Norma's Aunt being sick. She had cancer. Now Cale felt awful.

Cale walked over to the office door. He knocked with the same light knuckle tap he'd used last year. That time he had damaged the hallway ceiling with a football.

"Yes?" a voice came from inside.

Cale opened the door and looked in.

"Cale, come in." Principal Saunders' voice was grave.

Cale entered the office. Principal Saunders was sitting behind his huge desk, three chairs facing him. Behind him John Saunders kept books ranging from the classics to modern child psychology journals.

"Please sit down." John Saunders said to the teenager.

Cale did so in silence. He wondered how much trouble he and Randy were going to catch. It was obvious now that Randy hadn't done such a great job impersonating his mother.

"Cale," John Saunders sighed, "I don't know how to say this, and I'm sorry, I have to."

Had they found out about the blowjob? Were they going to expel him over a blowjob? His father was going to kill him. Good thing his dad already knew about that bomb.

"Sir?" Cale knew being polite was the route to take.

John Saunders sighed and said quietly. "There was

an accident this morning that involved your parents."

Cale gulped hard. "Are they hurt?" He could barely get the words out.

"I'm sorry." John knew the next words were going to change Cale O'Rourke's life. "Cale, your parents have been…your parents have passed away. They were…killed."

Cale bit his lip. He blinked. The room began to change dimensions.

"No, I was talking to my dad a couple hours ago." This was impossible, there had to be some kind of mistake.

"I'm sorry Cale. It happened about eight-thirty this morning."

Cale started to breath hard. "Mom and dad. Both?" Tears started to well in his eyes. He felt very scared. This wasn't supposed to happen in real life. Movies, TV, books and other people, but not to him. He looked around the room for something to focus on. He saw a teaching certificate. Cale started to read it.

John Saunders saw Cale trying to distract himself. He spoke softly.

"Yes, Cale. Both of them."

"I don't believe this." Cale felt tears blurring his vision. "It can't be true." Suddenly his cheeks were wet. He couldn't stop the tears, so he wiped them away strongly.

John Saunders buzzed Norma Alne. It had been decided earlier it would be best she took him out of school to see Dr. Paul Jensen. The doctor would be at the hospital, where Cale's parent's bodies were.

Cale looked up at her as she entered and took a deep breath.

Calm down. This is not how the folks would want you to be.

17

He stood up, taking two more deep breaths. He brushed back his bangs casually, but he found himself breathing like he had just come off a cross-country run.

Norma came up to him and hugged his heaving chest. She had known Cale all his life and he was glad she was near.

"Cale I'm so sorry."

"Norma, can I get out of here? Can I go see if it really was my folks?"

She nodded her head, then looked at John Saunders. The protocol was to wait for the board child psychiatrist, but John Saunders had always considered himself more human than bureaucrat. Seeing Paul Jensen was the right thing to do.

"Norma, why don't you and Mr. Ryder take Cale to the hospital. Cale you know Mr. Ryder from the guidance department?"

Cale pulled away from Norma. "I know Mr. Ryder. Thanks Mr. Saunders."

"Cale, I want you to see Dr. Jensen when you're there."

"I'm O.K.," Cale said, brushing tears away. Inside he was crumbling but without thinking he added, "And I'm sorry about yesterday. I …I skipped school."

"Cale, don't worry about that." Saunders and Norma Alne exchanged a quick glance. She was starting to cry again.

"Listen now, I'm supposed to keep you here until the right guardian can be reached. But if I send you to see a doctor, I can let you go to the hospital with Norma. It's got to happen this way, Cale." John wanted to see Cale checked for shock. He respected the boy's composure under the circumstances, but how long could it last?

John Saunders continued speaking, "Paul Jensen - Dr. Jensen, knew your father quite well, right?"

Cale nodded. *'Uncle'* Paul Jensen had played poker with his dad once or twice a month, on Thursday evenings since as far back as he could remember. Uncle Paul would be a good person to be around.

"Then it's settled", the principal said rubbing his eyes. He felt very sorry for Cale O' Rourke.

Cale didn't say much as he signed out. He reacted with a blank stony stare as office staff offered their sympathy. He focused on being able to see Paul Jensen. Walking out to the parking lot with Norma, he thought about his dad laughing with a big cigar in his mouth, while he played poker with his buddies. He prayed intensely, asking God for this to be a colossal mistake.

It was a blur for Cale until arriving at the small hospital. They entered walking past the administration desk and through emergency to the elevators. Norma knew where to go. In the elevator there was a man sitting in a wheelchair and a uniformed African American who was obviously his guard, standing behind him. The man in the wheelchair had handcuffs on watched the elevator doors close and then turned suddenly to Cale. He had long stringy hair and a blond beard stained from nicotine. He was wearing a backless hospital gown and clutching his left side.

"I got stabbed, boy. How 'bout you?" His voice was rough and his mouth partly hidden by the scraggly, unkempt beard. The large guard looked down with distaste at the man, but stayed silent.

19

"I was told my parents were just killed in a car accident. I'm here to make sure it's true." Cale's voice cracked a bit but he didn't cry. Norma started to sob and put her hand to her face.

"Sorry to hear it." The bearded man in the wheelchair looked back to the elevator doors. The rest of the ride was silent.

Paul Jensen met them at the door to his office. He was wearing a face Cale had never seen: extreme sadness. He overheard Norma tell Paul she would wait until it was decided where Cale was spending the night.

Cale had no idea what was going to happen. None of his nearby relatives were alive. His closest aunt lived in Canada. Cale wondered if he was old enough to live on his own.

Runaways. Runaways should get more respect because they have what it takes to live on their own. Do I?

"Cale, let's go into my office." Paul Jensen said quietly.

Cale nodded.

Upon entering, Cale went to the black leather sofa next to Paul's desk.

"I'm really sorry Cale."

"Are they really dead, Uncle Paul?" Cale gulped out. He was not going to breakdown again.

"They aren't here on Earth any more Cale." Paul sighed. "I want to make sure you know, myself, and a lot of others are going to do their best to look out for you until everything can be settled."

Cale blinked back a tear. "Thank you." Then he asked, "Am I going to have to leave my home?"

This is crazy.

Cale's face began to sag. His normally chiseled features looked dazed, his mouth hanging open slightly.

"Cale, I can't begin to tell you how proud your parents were of you."

Paul Jensen looked from Cale to the surface of his desk.

Cale thought this statement ironic given yesterday's circumstances. He hadn't even gotten the chance to tell his mother he was sorry for making her worry.

"I know they thought of provisions for you future."

"Provisions?" Things were getting more and more confusing.

"Cale, your father and I played poker with Russell Thomas, your family's lawyer, quite a lot. He's a good guy. I know Mr. Thomas will be able to answer many of your questions."

"How did they die?" It was the first time Cale asked. He wanted to change the subject of what the future was going to bring.

"A deer ran into your parents car. The deer went into the windshield and well… there was nothing anyone could do. They both died on the spot."

"A fucking deer?" Cale didn't curse around elders, but the words came out almost involuntarily. He tried to correct himself, "I mean, a deer killed them?"

"Yes. Deer, unfortunately, are responsible for a lot of road casualties."

Cale looked down to the ground as he remembered his father's last words. He told himself he would keep the promise to his father about telling the truth, no matter what.

"A deer." He looked up to Paul Jensen's face and gave a wry smile and brushed back another single tear.

"It's hard for me to believe too. Your father was a good friend. I know he would have wanted you to know the truth as soon as possible."

"*Would have wanted...*" Cale looked out the window. His face had taken on a drawn, beaten appearance. *Past tense was used a lot when people die,* Cale thought.

Paul Jensen leaned forward, concerned, "The truth is not always easy to face. " Paul Jensen rubbed his forehead as he softly spoke, "Or talk about. Sadly, you are being forced to get the courage to face a terrible truth at a very early age."

Taichung City
Taiwan, R.O.C

She wanted to be caressed this time, but she was a physically strong woman and needed to be dominated as well. After their clothes were off, she stared down at him with hungry eyes while his hands roamed over her body. Her legs were wrapped around his naked torso as he kissed her breasts. Suddenly he picked her up and walked to the shower.

They washed each other and Cale noticed she had a gentle touch, like most of the Asian women he'd been with. But Monica was very athletic. Hard bodied.

"To bedroom." She said. They made it to the bed kissing in silence. Cale went down on her as she stretched out and opened her legs. It was the beginning of sex that lasted three hours. Afterwards, while they talked, she smoked a cigarette.

"You are sexy!" She was speaking to him from the bed; Cale was in the bathroom cleaning up.

"Sorry, I can't understand your English!" They both laughed as Cale walked back into the bedroom.

"Get my purse for me."

Cale strutted naked in front of the mirrored doors of the walk-in closet, stopping to inspect the scratches she'd left. He smiled in the knowledge he had given her one hell of a ride.

Cale approached her with the small Louis Vutton clutch. She took out ten thousand NT dollars and handed it to him, still smoking the cigarette. It was the standard price for a specimen like Cale.

"Thanks." She smiled.

"No. Thank you, Monica." Cale bent down to kiss her on the forehead. She looked up at him suspiciously, then smiled and reached into her purse and pulled out five thousand more.

"What's this for?"

"You know. Shou fei. (Tip.)"

CHAPTER 3

Las Vegas, Nevada
(Five Years Ago)

Vesper Hu looked around her. This party was bigger than she had imagined. There were thousands of people in the convention center of the hotel.

She took a sip of her drink, a mojito. The club was promoting rum based drinks. It was a little sweeter than she liked her mojitos. Not enough mint. She took another sip as a large man in an expensive suit bumped into her.

"Excuse me." She said, smiling up at him over her straw.

"Oh, hey. Sorry, there, baby." His solid yellow tie was slightly askew. *American men were so dangerous when they drank. And so large!*

She examined herself looking down her front; her black cocktail dress was still spotless. Vesper kept in a little yawn. She was getting antsy. It seemed last year's Nightclub and Bar Show had been much more interesting. Vesper admitted to herself, she wasn't used to standing alone. Nobody seemed to take any notice of her.

"Look at these guys go!" A tall blond woman in a manager's suit spoke from beside her. Seeing Vesper holding back her yawn the woman asked loudly, "Are you bored or something? Look at the bodies up there! Look at that guy, he's a fucking superman!" She was now shouting to be heard over the music. "Do they have this kind of dancing in Japan?" Her breath had a heavy gin smell that lingered, even in the crowded club.

"I don't know. I am from Taiwan." Vesper decided to be friendly. She extended her hand and said louder, "My name is Vesper."

"Oh, I'm Nancy. I'm from Wyoming." Nancy Marshall took the hand and the two women smiled at each other. The tall woman leaned down and put a hand to her mouth, "They definitely don't have guys like that dancing on stages in Wyoming." She raised her gin and tonic to point at a male dancer alone on a single podium.

Vesper saw him for a moment before he disappeared behind a wall of giants. "We don't have this kind of thing in Taiwan. We are much too conservative. You are here for the convention?" She could tell Nancy was not paying attention. Nancy's eyes were on the stage.

"Yea." Nancy was starting to move her body to the beat, still staring towards the podium. She turned and gave Vesper a quick smile, "I'm in F&B. Laramie Hilton." Then she turned back to the stage. Nancy seemed hypnotized by the podium.

"I'm here to purchase wine." Vesper said to finalize the conversation.

"He is so fucking hot – and he's taking off his…shirt! Excuse me, I have to get closer to this." Nancy pushed her way into the crowd ahead, drink in hand, following the lead of quite a few other ladies. Every one of them seemed taller and bigger than Vesper. She looked around the walls of the club and started to make her way to the stairs. The upper floors of the place would make for better viewing.

Vesper Hu owned twenty-three clubs in Taiwan that catered to female customers. Ladies who didn't like to consume alcohol in public bars. Women, who wanted discretion about how they enjoyed their good times. In Taiwan, her type of establishment was quite common for the male patron, but clubs that catered to female clientele exclusively were rare and extremely profitable. Vesper knew in order to continue being sanctuaries for females with readily disposable income, her clubs had to stay exclusive. She spent top dollar and she got top dollar back.

Vesper found the stairs and made her way up to an open landing with a good view of the stage. Two gigantic bouncers stood monitoring the flow of people, waving stragglers along with polite authority. Vesper took out one of the hundred dollar bills she kept for this very thing.

"Excuse me, I'm not so tall as you Americans, and I'd like to watch from here." Vesper said with a smile as she handed over the bill. The stone-faced bouncer moved aside with no hesitation, without even looking at her, taking the money and directing her to the railing behind him.

In the center of the venue, there were four white podiums, with one dancer on each; two males, two females. Vesper now had a commanding view of the whole scene.

The music was inspiring neither Vesper, nor the dancers to do much to the beat. It was Trance so it was almost ethereal. Not what this party needed to keep hopping. She looked for Nancy, now lost in a sea of party people. This was becoming thoroughly boring, although the male dancers were definitely hot.

She took a sip of her drink as she appraised the males. The black one had a good muscular body. Vesper looked over at the white male who had very blonde hair. He was closest to the stairs and Vesper reveled in her position. She took another sip of her mojito as she stared down at the blonde man. She was close enough to see his facial expression. Despite his constant motion, he was smiling seductively.

The music changed. She recognized this, Eminem. Or was it Slim Shady? It didn't really matter, the girls back home liked him, so she knew of his music. The blonde dancer without a shirt had a well-developed body. He had the abdominals of an underwear model. No hair. Vesper liked hairless.

He was now pointing at someone on the floor, still moving his body, rotating his hips in a sexual manner. His moves were making her forget her surroundings. He had caught a hidden rhythm in the song and was exploiting it with professional dance moves. He seemed supremely confident. Vesper liked this.

His blond hair was damp from sweating to the beat. The crowd kept pushing to surround his podium. Vesper looked at the faces raised up to this man, watching him. This Adonis seemed to feed off the attention.

Vesper leaned over the glass railing. As the mesmerizing man rotated, she eyed his profile intently. His beautiful face reminded her of the best statues she had seen in Florence. She was pulled out of this fantasy as he started to pump his fist in the air. The crowd cheered and many threw their fists in the air in unison.

He looked up and caught Vesper staring down at

him. It was only for an instant, but he managed to slip a wink in for her benefit. Vesper knew she would have to meet this man. She felt a pleasant warm ache creep through her belly.

Vesper appraised the body closer; the chest had parted pectorals with a waist tapered to a desirable V. His physique was archetypal. Vesper felt another involuntary flash inside her. He was causing this. There was no denying it.

The eyes of the crowd followed his every move and he leapt in the air as they roared with enthusiasm. As Vesper scanned the throngs of people she noticed that almost everyone was mimicking him by jumping in time with his actions. She had never seen this type of behavior before.

Remembering Nancy's reaction, Vesper smiled as she caught herself formulating some kind of plan to get this specimen back to Taiwan. He had a physical magnetism that was very attractive to her. From the look of the females in the crowd, she doubted she was the only one entertaining these types of thoughts.

His hands roamed his body. Vesper licked her lips involuntarily. There was some commotion on the stairs behind her as the bouncers jostled a loud drunk out. Vesper didn't turn around.

Money wouldn't be the problem. A serious relationship could present a barrier, but what Vesper wanted, Vesper usually got. She continued to watch him. There was no mistaking it, he had some magic that made a woman feel weak. Suddenly the song was over and he was getting down off the stage

From her vantage point on the landing, Vesper saw the dancers who left the podium standing around a heavy-set man at the side of the stage behind some large sound equipment. The fat man was yelling at her objective.

"Yeah, whatever." Ralph continued, he was getting red in the face, "Nick, you are one of the best dancers I've ever seen. You're hot, you got a great body. But dude, the hoops you make people go through just because you're great, man, it isn't worth it."

"This crowd likes it well enough." They were yelling at each other to be heard above the din. Nick wiped the sweat off of his chest with his bare hands. His brown eyes were full of contempt for Ralph.

What the hell did this fat bastard know about dancing? The Ralph was a total 'Mo', but the artistic gene was non-existent. Why was this guy still breathing?

"Nick, I'm fucking through with this shit. You're fired." Everyone at the Stardust who knew him called him *"The Ralph"*. The only guys that got along with The Ralph were the guys that let him suck up, literally. The Ralph liked his boys obedient and willing. Nick had disliked the guy from day one.

Nick Young looked at the older man with disdain. He got right in Ralph Marin's face knowing it would drive the guy over the edge. There were other jobs available.

"I'd say "blow me", Ralph, but your fat ass would probably suck my dick right here."

Ralph Marin was furious. This was worse than when Nick had called him a "Curry Queen" in front of a few dancers last week. "You...you know, you are a piece of work, rebel-boy. Your-way-or-no-way has gotten you...the highway." The Ralph snapped his fingers to dismiss him. "Find some other poor person to torment."

The Ralph seemed on the verge of tears but he was attempting to maintain his authority in front of the other dancers.

"Fine." A drop of sweat fell from Nick's chin. He pushed his pale blond hair back. "Your loss, Curry Queen."

Nick picked up his shirt and began to put it on. Neither one noticed the demure Asian woman watching the scene intently from the landing above.

"Just get the fuck out of here, Backstreet Boy. Now!" Ralph Marin hissed, turning away from Nick. He looked towards a tall black male dancer standing close by toweling himself off. "Mark, go to stage three where Nick is supposed to be. This song is ending. No improv shit."

Mark looked at Nick. They knew each other from prior gigs and got along well, but this crowd was warmed up. Maybe Nick could afford to lose this job, he seemed be in constant demand as a dancer. Mark had auditioned for a month to get this job. He'd only been selected last week. This was Las Vegas, friendships counted but jobs were king.

"Get'em, Mark. Your turn." Nick said, putting on his jacket. He leaned in so both men could hear him, "Word of advice though," he looked into Ralph Marin's eyes as he spoke, "Watch out for this homo. He's desperate." He put on a Yankee's baseball cap and turned away before Ralph could react and pushed his way through a gaggle of blonds at the side of the stage.

The high he had felt moments ago on stage was gone. All the faces that had been locked on his dancing performance were now smiling and staring at someone else. Nick sighed to himself. During his "controversial" time on stage, he let the rhythm inside tell him how to move. He hadn't felt more alive or tuned in since… Nick stopped himself. He wasn't going to let his train of thought continue. It was time to move on. He pulled the baseball cap tighter over his sweaty hair and headed for the doors of the club. The DJ heated the crowd up for yet another b-boy peak. The beat was building over the long exaggerated twang of an electric guitar note. It was building, all the bass gone, high-hats layering in over the guitar note as a funky electric riff began. As he approached the exits, the song began to reach another crescendo. Nick turned around. Looking up at Mark, he smiled. The guy had decent moves, but nothing outstanding. A few practiced dance maneuvers. Nick searched the stage area for The Ralph. Catching the fat man's eye for an instant, Nick gave him a larger-than-life, boy-scout salute.

"You are much better than him." The voice surprised Nick from his left side. How had she gotten so close to him without him noticing? Her perfume had not preceded her presence, but now it spoke volumes. This woman was rich. He drank her in, inhaling deeply, unabashedly, as he tilted his head a bit to get a better look at her.

She smiled at him, eyes, not head, tilted slightly up to him. Vesper knew she wasn't young, but she still had a slim, tight body and her smile had always been disarming. She had succeeded in her business by fully understanding the male psyche. Specifically, the psyche of confident, handsome men.

"Thanks." Nick Young nodded to her. She was hot. Getting on in age, but hot. Exotic. The woman got even closer and extended her hand.

"I'm Vesper." Nick took her hand. It was elegant,

31

dainty and with some serious bling.

"Hi Vesper, thanks for the compliment." He wasn't ready to say his name.

"Not a compliment, a fact." They were jostled together as a crowd of fresh customers surged in from the entrance.

"What sort of name is Vesper?" Nick looked at the throng of people heading in from the main casino area.

"I'm Taiwanese and Irish American. My American father picked my English name out of a cocktail book. There is a martini called the vesper." She laughed playfully as though it was the first time she'd explained this.

Nick could tell by her accent she did not live in America.

Don't' forget to buy cigarettes on the way home.

"My name gets so much attention here in Las Vegas." She rubbed her right eye slightly, batting her eyelashes. "So annoying."

Nick liked this woman.

Pretty fresh package for an exotic, rich cougar. The Asian ones are usually so shy.

"Vesper martini. Never had one. I'll have to try it sometime." Nick chuckled a little. Her composure in his presence was refreshing. Despite the dim lighting of the club Nick could see she was ageless in that mysterious Oriental way.

"The vesper is not for everyone. It is very strong." Before Nick could react she leaned in, standing on her toes to speak directly into his left ear. "It wasn't a random name." Nick felt her breath touch his earlobe. Her perfume was even better up close. "The vesper martini has a history my father liked." Vesper pulled away to give him a spirited look, so close they could have kissed.

"History?" Nick grinned.

Vesper stirred the last of her mojito while she stared into his eyes, "The vesper martini was named after a female spy in *Casino Royale*, the James Bond book. They even put out a bad movie of this story. Sadly, it didn't star a good James Bond." She licked her lips. "Anyway, the vesper martini didn't exist until James Bond introduced it."

"James Bond created a martini?"

"Yes. Well, really Ian Flemming made up the drink's name. Apparently, he liked martinis."

"Is he the bad guy in the movie?" Nick didn't go to movies often. As far as watching a James Bond flick went, it either had Sean Connery or he didn't care. He had not seen the *Casino Royale* movie nor had he read a Bond book.

Vesper laughed. Nick looked at the entrance again. He was wet with sweat and getting uncomfortable. *The Ralph* would sick someone on him if he stuck around much longer.

Vesper spoke quickly with impeccable English, "No, Flemming was the author. The story is Bond falls for a secret agent named, Vesper Lynd. He names a type of martini after her before she betrays him and is killed." Vesper licked her lips again.

"Quite a story." Nick commented, straining to hear her over the music.

"I think it's interesting that the last thing James Bond had to say about her was, "The bitch is dead now." Literally, it is the last line of the book. After that he never drank another vesper martini." Vesper laughed again, sweeping her hair in a way that provided Nick with a fresh dose of her perfume.

"Your father had a strange sense of humor," Nick was surprisingly at ease with this stranger, but the need to leave was beginning to grow now.

"Maybe he knew what I was going to turn into."

"A double agent?" Nick gave a little laugh.

"Maybe. I think I have the look." Vesper struck a sultry pose, her hair hiding half her face.

"Ya, you do." Nick nodded, smiling as he turned to look back at the stage. Ralph Marin was staring at him red with anger. When he saw Nick looking at him he turned to speak with one of the security guards near the stage.

"So should I ask you about your name or not?" Vesper's voice purred.

Nick answered with a smile knowing he had to depart. "Vesper, I'm Nick. It's been a pleasure to meet you, but I've got to get out of here before I'm asked to leave."

"If you're not going back up, I'm not staying."

Nick found himself smiling again.

"I'm not going back up."

"Can I ask you a favor then?" Vesper lightly licked her lips knowing full well the effect it had on men.

"Sure." Nick spoke hesitantly. He was pretty sure he knew what was coming next.

"I'm a little hungry, and I want to go to a really nice restaurant I've read about." She paused and looked directly into his eyes, "I don't want to eat alone, and I find myself in the company of the best dancer in Las Vegas. I have to ask; will you have dinner with me? "

Nick smiled and nodded, "Wish I could, but I've got

stuff to do. Maybe we can do it another time. Why don't you give me your number?" She was tempting, but he didn't want to be around anyone at the moment.

Vesper continued to look into his smiling face,

"Nick, have you ever thought about living outside of the United States?"

Nick was taken aback. "No. Not really."

"Please, do us both a favor and come to dinner. I saw that fat gross man yelling at you and that never has to happen again."

"So what are you recruiting me for? Do I get to be a double agent?" Nick looked into her eyes. He was interested.

"Nick, all you need to know about me, is I'm Vesper Hu, not Vesper Lind." She didn't blink as she spoke. "Trust me, you haven't begun to live yet."

CHAPTER 4

Kuta Beach, Bali
Indonesia

"I know you said 'no'. But that was before, mate. This is really important now. I really need you to do this for me or I'm fucked." The voice was low and pleading. Gary Pierce wasn't used to begging.

"Gary, I really can't. You're my best mate and it's hard to say no, but I can't." Cale choked out the last words. He didn't want to say no but his back was against the wall.

"I could go to jail when we get back." Gary was done beseeching. He stared intently at Cale. His voice still held a tone of disbelief.

Cale could tell he was not going to let this go.

"Why did you say you were with me?" Cale scratched his head and stood up. He started to pace the bungalow they were sharing with Gary's girlfriend and Helena. He was conscious of the fact he was avoiding Gary's penetrating eyes.

"Cale, I didn't have any choice. Believe me, I wouldn't have said it, but I was in a spot and … I thought you'd back me up. I'd do it for you."

"I wouldn't ever ask you to lie for me." Cale said, forcing himself to look into Gary's eyes. They stared at each

36

other, each man so sure they were justified; they felt like strangers to the other.

"Cale, she doesn't even remember what the fuck happened. I'll get blamed because she had slapped me earlier at the party in front of people. This bitch is crazy."

Cale walked to the small refrigerator to grab a beer.

"She was so bizarre Cale, after Tina left with her friends and I fucked off down the street, she thought she could find me and spit more venom at me. She followed me down the goddamn street like a fucking stalker. A drunken fucked up female stalker. I tell her to piss off, she leaves and goes and gets her self beat up some how." Gary sighed deeply, then he continued, "Now, I'm accused because I'm the only person she can remember seeing last. To the friggin' campus police, it's a fucking textbook case. They've got motive, witnesses to our argument and she only remembers me and her fighting." He counted off on his fingers. "She's probably got my DNA under her finger nails from the fucking walloping she gave me." Gary's voice got quieter. "Cale, I couldn't go to the police without an alibi. I don't have any idea how the fuck she got beat up. I really don't, but I panicked and said I was with you at the time." Gary's voice was almost a whisper. "I need your help, mate."

"Why didn't you tell me right away you were in this much trouble? You waited until we're on holiday! This was over four days ago! How did you even get out of the country?"

"Cale, it's still a campus police thing right now. Still small time."

"You need a fucking lawyer more than you need me to make bullshit up."

"Cale, I waited because we'd already planned Bali three months ago and I thought it would be a great opportunity…" Gary finally looked away from him as his voice got quieter. "… to work on our story."

Gary was starting to cry. His voice was still even, but tears were running down his cheeks.

"Is that what back-up means to you? Lying? Have you ever known me to lie before, Gary?" Cale shut his eyes. None of this would have happened if Gary didn't have such a reputation for fighting. There was no way Gary had assaulted his ex. Cale knew it, anyone who knew Gary would. He was a gentleman to the ladies and while he had moved on with a great girl, Tina, his ex had turned into a psycho. The trouble was, Gary was correct about one thing. To the campus police it would seem like a textbook case of revenge.

"I was in a pinch, mate. I had to give them something when they came to my door. She can't remember anything except arguing with me. So she wakes up with a broken face and a few less teeth and is already pissed at me." Gary raised his voice and stood up. He was now staring at Cale in an unfamiliar way, a way Cale would not recognize until later as wide-eyed fear. "All you have to do is say I was with you around midnight."

"I want to help, but there's got to be a better way. If I lie for you it will just make things worse. And you know how I am – I can't lie. So, let's figure out another way." Cale crossed his arms.

"But Cale, I already said I was with you. I'm dog meat if you don't help me on this."

"Gary…" Cale sighed, "The point is, I wasn't with

you. I wasn't home!"

"Cale, please, goddamn it. I need this. I'll do anything. I'll owe you forever." He was looking intently at Cale again. There was no hint of his usual sarcasm. "I'll make it up to you any way I can." Gary's mouth started to actually hang open a bit in incredulity his mate was saying no.

Cale shook his head, "Wrong guy." He said, again forcing himself to look into Gary's eyes.

Gary stood up. He looked at the man before him, "Whatever turned you against me, I hope something happens to change you back. I mean, really, my heart is heavy. Maybe I fucked up by jumping the gun a bit with my story, but I thought you were my friend."

"I am your friend." Cale said, looking at the ground.

"No, Cale. You're the guy who's going to let the real criminal get-off, and allow Gary Pierce to be thrown out of school! Maybe go to jail, definitely have his life ruined. You're being no friend at all, mate. Can't you see that?"

Cale stood and watched as Gary started for the door, grabbing his wallet from the small plain dresser in the middle of the room.

"Gary."

"I just need to be away from you, mate." Gary turned and walked out of the bungalow.

Cale looked at himself in the mirror. He felt wronged. He wasn't heartless. Of course he wanted to help but the promise to his father hung in his mind like a Shakespearean ghost. As difficult as the situation was, one thing was sure for Cale: the truth was not up for compromise.

Gary walked back into the room, "Tina and I are off to the Sari Club." Gary cleared his throat, "Don't think I want you around me tonight, so maybe that's one place to steer clear of, alright?"

"Gary, I wish you could know how sorry I am that I can't help you the way you want me to. If..." Cale's voice was low and Gary almost relished cutting him off as he stood in the doorway,

"Not sorry enough, mate." Gary slammed the door shut, leaving his final words to echo in Cale O'Rourke's head. A minute later Cale heard him leave with Tina.

Cale stood silent as Helena Huang came into the room brushing her hair. She looked at her boyfriend questioningly.

"What was that all about?"

"Gary wants me to lie to help him."

"Lie?"

"Yeah, Trudy Jacobs is saying he beat her up."

"Trudy Jacobs? That bloody cunt!" Helena stopped brushing her long black hair. "She's a fucking loser."

Cale smiled a little at his lover's words. Helena didn't use strong language unless she was really upset.

"Don't hold back your feelings, babe." Cale walked past her and sat on the bed. "I hate telling Gary no, but I'm not going to lie for him. It won't help the situation, it never does."

"I know about your promise, Cale."

"Gary acts like it is no big deal."

"It is a big deal, but Gary is in a bad situation if that woman is involved. I know her. She has a black heart. I'm not surprised someone beat her up."

"Doesn't justify me lying."

"Cale, I understand how you feel. I admire you. You

40

don't lie, O.K., but this is your best friend's life!"

"Doesn't matter. A lie is a lie."

"Why are you being like this? I can't believe you're being so...so fucking stubborn." She had never sworn at him before.

"Helena, this is my life we are talking about too."

"Cale, you are being so silly. Your father would never want you to turn down a friend in need. It's called a white lie because there's nothing bad about it. It can help. Your father would understand the circumstances." She sounded exasperated.

"I don't know about that. And I'm getting pretty fucking sick of you telling me what my Dad would expect from me. I know what he would say. And I know what I'm saying now. I'm not going to lie for Gary. He doesn't need me to anyway. There's got to be a better way. It would just make it a little easier for him if I lied. That's no reason to lie to the police."

Helena stormed into the bathroom. He heard running water.

"Gary's life could be screwed because you can't be..."

"Be what?" He was yelling now. With the water running he didn't know if she could hear him.

Helena came to the door of the simple bathroom, "Be reasonable. Gary could go to jail."

In an instant, he was angrier with her than he'd ever been. "If it came to that then I would help him. But this is bullshit. Why am I getting all this hostility from you? You could try a little harder to understand my position."

Helena came out of the bathroom. In the back of his

mind he noted she had put on her make-up.

"Would you be so stubborn if it was one of your children?" Helena asked quietly.

"Gary isn't my kid!" Cale's voice was loud and harsh. "And he's not yours either!"

"What if it was me in Gary's situation? Wait. Never mind. I don't want to know the answer to that question."

"That's not fair!" Cale shouted. He could smell her perfume as she moved towards him in anger.

"Yes it is!" Helena shouted back. "You talk about these values your parents gave you. I'm just curious, would you lie to keep me out of jail?"

"Why are you being such a bitch? What kind of question is that?" Cale wanted this conversation to stop.

Why did she have perfume on?

"Cale, what would you do if I needed you like Gary does now?" Her voice had gotten lower.

"I don't know Helena. Why are you even asking me?"

"Because you have to help Gary."

"I'm not lying for him." Cale looked straight into Helena's eyes.

Helena shook her head.

"I love you with all my heart, Cale O'Rourke, but right now you are being a petulant child." Her voice got quieter as she continued. "I'm going to find Tina and Gary, and say how sorry I am. Sorry that I have a boyfriend who thinks this way."

"Well maybe you don't need a fucking boyfriend like me then." Cale said as fury started to dominate his emotions.

They stared at each other, furious. "I don't need a

fucking…" Helena paused in mid sentence. "I will go now."
She said with a determined smile. Her voice was steady.

"Then go. They went to the Sari Club." Cale turned
away from her. "I hope you all have a great time because
I promise I won't be there to spoil it." Cale walked away
to the bedroom and didn't look back. He heard her go out
the front door.

An hour later he heard several blasts of thunder that
rocked the town of Kuta Beach. Cale had heard the noise
from inside the bungalow and went out. A couple guys
from the next bungalow were milling about.

"What was that?" he asked a younger man wearing
only boxer shorts.

"Don't know mate, our buddy just went down the
street." They looked in the direction of the massive sound.
"He's got a cell phone and Jack over there has his. We'll find
out in a few minutes."

"It was loud whatever it was." Cale said looking to
the horizon. It was hard to see anything above the tall trees
that surrounded the bungalow compound.

"Woke me up. Me and most of my mates are knack-
ered from the games today."

"Games?"

"Ah mate, this is championships for football, Asian
regionals."

"It's amateur, isn't it?"

"Break my heart. It's championships."

The cell phone rang. Cale looked over. He was curious.

"Fuck no!" the footballer holding the phone
screamed. He looked all around him stricken and tearing-

up like a child. Then he said, "Those were bombs! Bombs just went off down the road in some clubs. Aaron says there's blood and bodies everywhere."

Cale went numb.

This can't be happening.

Without saying a word, Cale ran down the narrow street leading to the Sari Club.

An hour later, Cale found himself identifying the first of his travel companions for the authorities. He had found Gary's corpse smoldering in the gutter. The body was lying beside three others that were dead in the street. Only the torso, right arm and head were attached. The face, blackened and blistered was shocking. The hair had been cooked into a blackened matt. Cale started crying on the spot. His tears fell silently. Gary's dilemma existed no longer.

He helped transport bodies away from the scene amidst the ridiculous confusion of the authorities. He found Tina about three hours after the explosion. He recognized her blouse. Confirming it was Tina, her passport had been in her front shorts pocket. Her face was unrecognizable.

At dawn, Cale found Helena's dead body at a make-shift clinic. Both of her legs were missing. Cale's eyes were so sore from the black soot in the air his tears were a relief.

He was walking away from the clinic when he ran into his neighbor from the bungalow complex, who was now dressed in filthy tan shorts and a blue singlet. There was blood all over his hands. Cale looked down at his own clothing. He also had bloodstains.

"It's a mess, isn't it?"

"Unbelievable."

"You know anybody who was in it?"

"Everyone I came here with."

"Ah, mate. Were you with the Taipei team? I heard almost all of them bought it."

Cale shook his head. "No. My girlfriend and two other friends. None survived."

The footballer was stunned but angry, "I just met a guy who lost his kid brother and sister. I can't fathom how some assholes could do this."

"They know who did it?"

"It's all rumor right now. But the one I'm hearing most is Bin Laden's guys."

Cale shook his head.

"Mate, I got to run. I'm sorry about your girlfriend. All the best."

Cale was dead tired, but knew the next step was to get in touch with each family. He didn't have any idea what to say. "Hi, this is Cale O'Rourke and because I got in a fight with Gary and Helena, the whole lot went to the Sari Club to be away from me. Now they're dead and I'm alive."

Cale made a decision then. He wasn't going back to Australia. He wasn't sure what he was going to do with his life as he walked back to the bungalow in a daze. He found himself hoping he would be unable to find the family's contact numbers in his friend's belongings. Unfortunately, he did.

After reaching all three families, he was desperate to get off this cursed island, but the airport was a zoo, and he had told all on the phone he would wait until they came to retrieve the bodies.

Cale didn't hang around his bungalow that next day. He went into the interior of Bali to Ubud. He drove to scenic spots in his Lonely Planet book on Bali. The locals were agitated and he was stopped several times by police. He eventually found himself next to an inland lake, tears falling as he stared out at the open water for several hours.

When the families did arrive, there never seemed an opportune moment to tell the true series of events. Cale had inferred he hadn't been feeling up to going out to the Sari Club with the group, and that was what had saved his life. They all said the same thing, it wasn't his fault, don't feel guilty for being lucky. Cale knew better.

Right. Lucky.

Cale had no one he could tell about the fights that had occurred, but he knew he had to. He had to come clean. Especially concerning the argument with Helena. It had to be someone who would understand the love he had for his girlfriend.

Even at the airport, days later, he was still unsure of where to go. He wasn't going to use the return ticket. He walked by the booths for China Air. Cale was reminded of how many people had died from the Taipei football club.

Such a waste.

Then it hit him. Taiwan was where Helena's grandmother lived. She was the person he could tell and set the record straight. Spontaneously, he walked to the counter and bought a ticket on the next plane to Taipei.

CHAPTER 5

Taipei City
Taiwan, R.O.C.
October 16, 2002

Cale tried to focus. He'd been awake for the entire six-hour flight from Bali even though he'd had little sleep for the past five days. He was grateful for the automatic walkway in the arrival area. A pink orchid and a beautiful Asian woman's face smiled a welcome from a huge poster. He wasn't exactly sure what it was trying to sell. Then he saw it, in small font at the bottom: Long Wang Semi-Conductors.

The immigration hall was huge. The walls were massive windows looking outside to the terminal. It was raining. The languages buzzing around were alien. Cale saw a sign indicating the lines set aside for foreigners.

This is crazy.

He could have done this after final exams. He should be back in Australia. It would have been too much to go all the way home to Canada. Texas probably would have screwed him up more. As he waited in line for his turn at the immigration desk his mind drifted back to a conversation with Helena months ago last semester.

It was a Sunday. They had just finished their last set of exams and were enjoying a second day of holidays, lying in bed together. As a couple, they seemed to spend most of their time in the bedroom.

"I want us to travel. I want us to go to Europe together. Or somewhere." Helena stared at his chest, stroking it gently with her fingers. Cale watched, fascinated by the delicate bone structure.

"You know, I don't really even like the physical act of traveling. Traveling is never easy. It's just the more you do it, the easier it gets." Cale stared at the ceiling. Remembering all the places he had called home, none felt so fitting as this small student room in Australia. At least since his parents had died.

"But don't you feel excited, you know, like you're going to see another land! You meet so many new people." She got so excited about traveling, and was envious of Cale's globe trotting.

"Yup, meeting new people makes the traveling part worth while."

"You know, I think traveling is easier if …" She turned her head to look at him, "If you like doing it. I think some people are not supposed to travel."

Cale grunted agreement.

"It's too bad. I guess planes, airports and stuff can be intimidating, but you only have to do it once or twice to become…accomplished."

Cale smiled. She was always hitting the thesaurus.

"You have to do it, like three times and then, it's easy."

"What? Traveling?" He continued to look at the ceiling as he ran his hand along her bare leg. "Or other stuff?"

"Aiyo!" She dragged out the eye oh.

He laughed as she convulsed with excitement at his touches. "What's aiyo?"

"It's Taiwanese. It's like aiyoo! Like, you know, hey! My parents say it all the time."

"Like, hey let's fuck?"

"You are so bad!" But she didn't argue as he began gentle foreplay.

When they had exhausted themselves, Cale left the room and returned quickly with glasses of water.

"Do you think of your parents often?" Helena Huong asked her lover as she drank deeply. Morning light filtered through his pale blue curtains.

"Almost every day." Cale whispered. She wasn't the first girlfriend to ask about his parents, but she was the most persistent.

"It still hurt much?" Helena set her water on a side table and moved into position for more chest teasing.

"Sure." Cale kept his voice quiet. It was a habit he had picked up during the group therapy sessions in high school. Not entirely out of reverence to his deceased parents; keeping his voice low seemed to invite fewer questions.

The air conditioner made a sleepy white noise. It was a great air-conditioner. She'd bought it for his birthday.

"I miss my grandmother." Helena's hand rested on his abdomen. They lay on top of the covers. "She is my idol."

"Really?"

"Uh-huh." A finger went gently into his belly button.

They sighed in unison.

"Yeah, she went through a lot. When she was eleven

she was raped by occupying soldiers."

"Japanese?"

"Not sure. Taiwan had it rough, though, and so did my grandmother. Colonized by Japan and then the home base for the KMT."

"KMT? What's that?"

"Do you know anything about Chinese history?"

"Why should I?"

"Well, for one thing, it is one of the oldest cultures in existence with over five thousand years of history. Now it is, once again, one of the most important cultures in the world." Helena loved talking politics. She was studying International Relations. Cale thought she needed to tone down her excitability. She sometimes had inflexible opinions.

"Those might be good reasons to learn about it." Then she moved closer and put her lips to his ears and whispered, "Plus you have a girlfriend whose ancestors are Chinese." Then she kissed his right ear lobe as she continued to whisper, "If you did learn, it would be so hot. I would love you forever."

"Forever?"

Helena pulled back and looked at his face. "My grandmother would love you – you're big and strong and smart. I can imagine myself going to her house with you and she would be so happy because she could talk to you in her language. Her English is O.K., but she would be really impressed by a foreigner that can speak Chinese." Her hairless legs cycled with genuine excitement, rubbing against his. She could never touch him enough.

"I guess now I know the secret weapon. Consider it

done. I'm going to learn Chinese. I can take an elective next semester." Cale's voice was husky. He hated languages but he loved this girl. He loved her so much more than his past girlfriends, he had decided a week ago to give her something special.

Helena shifted her weight into his body. "I love you." She kissed him tenderly, breathing heavy with passion. He loved the smell of her breath.

"I want you to have something." He'd been waiting almost a week to give it to her. Now seemed like the perfect moment. Cale jumped out of bed as she sat up on her knees.

"Yea! Present time!" She clapped her hands over her naked breasts.

Cale went to his dresser and took out a tiny, black, velvet box. Inside was a gold locket with a fine golden chain. This locket meant a lot to him.

"Oh my God! I love it. It's beautiful."

"It was my mother's. I was told to give it to a special lady."

"Really?" The tiny gold object hypnotized her as he opened the clasp and put it on.

"It's a special piece of jewelry, Helena."

They kissed briefly before she pushed him away playfully to inspect the locket further. She opened it up.

"There's no picture inside…" She was taken aback. "Why is there no picture?"

"You're supposed to put a picture in." Cale laughed heartily. "Imagine if I asked you to carry around a picture of my dead father!"

Helena swallowed, turning it over in her hands. "So

this was your mother's?"

"It was given to her by her older sister. Now it's yours." He was staring at the locket in her hands. She slowly let it slide down to hang between her healthy cleavage. It swung there, back and forth like a pendulum.

"Thank you, babe. I already know the picture of you I want to put in here."

Cale was interrupted from his thoughts by an accented male voice.

"Sir, please go to line for foreigners. This is incorrect line for you." The immigration official was smiling. It was a fake smile.

"Sorry."

He had found the locket on the bed table at their bungalow. It was in his travel bag with some other jewelry.

Following a crowd of Chinese, he had wandered into the wrong line. This really was a much larger airport than Denpasar in Bali.

Cale went to the longer, foreigner line. He shuffled ahead as the line moved. Cale looked around the immense hall. It could hold hundreds of travelers. Although the lines were not short, they were moving quickly. It explained why only half the booths were being used. He heard Tagalog and recognized the majority of the people in line as Filipino. They were all wearing a similar company uniform. They could have been a professional sports team. After a short wait, he found himself standing at the red line painted on the floor, watching the last person in front of him being processed.

Cale looked at his passport. It was American, but it looked strange in his hands. The United States and the memories associated were from a time that seemed long ago from another lifetime. It had been over a decade since he had resided in the U.S. Now only his finances did.

Cale's plan was to check into his hotel. Depending on the time he got settled, he would call Helena's grandmother and make arrangements to meet. He wasn't sure where Taichung was from the airport. If it was too late he would wait until tomorrow. That would even let him catch up on some sleep.

The person in front was cleared with a stamp from the immigration officer. Cale stepped forward as he sighed to himself.

"So, this is Taiwan."

CHAPTER 6

Taichung City
Taiwan, R.O.C.

The taxi dropped him at a narrow street with squat concrete houses built side by side. Cale had seen sidewalks bigger than this road. Except for a couple of potted trees there was no vegetation, just bleak grey walls with glass shards sprinkled on top. It seemed a very stark cityscape for a tropical country. The street seemed impossibly narrow, even for a one-way, but there were cars parked facing both directions. He paid the driver with two red currency notes and got out. Leaving the air-conditioning of the car he walked into a moist, oppressive wall of heat.

How old is this place? It's like a communist version of the Twilight Zone.

He looked down the small road. It was deserted. Skyscrapers in the background contrasted with the small concrete structures, bricks crumbling on the older homes he passed.

Cale searched for numbers on each building. He was grateful for the Roman numerals, almost everything else seemed alien.

The air was thicker than what he was used to. He hoped Helena's grandmother had air conditioning. The houses he passed had large stone gates and was unable to see in.

Helena's grandmother had been pleasant and kind on the phone. Plus, her English seemed pretty good. It would be much easier to communicate than he had originally thought. They had not talked long, but Cale had tried to convey what Helena had expressed months before as his reason for visiting.

Cale pressed the doorbell outside the gate of number 333. The high-pitched birdcall from the ringer was sharp and loud, and triggered a mixture of equally sharp emotions.

Get a grip. You're just tired.

He found himself looking down at his left foot. It was still.

The door to the gate opened and a young woman appeared.

"Hi, I'm Cale O'Rourke." Cale said haltingly. He had no idea who she was and started to doubt if he had the right address.

"Mister Cale?" *Mistah Gale.* Her smile was wide. It reminded him of the immigration officer's.

"Yes. Do you speak English?"

Please speak English.

"A little. But it's so poor! My English so poor." She said, forcing some laughter. Cale had never seen anyone smile so big.

"Your English is better than my Chinese. This is Mrs. Chen's house?"

"Yes. Mrs. Chen. Make a food. She make a food now."

"That's good." It was Cale's turn to smile.

The woman paused and told him, her smile fading a bit, "I am Annie. Neighbor."

"I guess you already know my name." They shook hands lightly. Then Annie pointed to some slippers just inside the door.

"You can wear. You can wear."

Cale took off his Adidas trainers. He thought this only happened in Japan. He put on the slippers and followed Annie into the house.

As Cale walked down the dim hallway the strong smell of incense overpowered the competing background ambience of steamed vegetables. He could taste the incense on his tongue.

I guess they don't have Frebreaze here yet.

Annie brought him to a sitting parlor. It was a separate room off the hall, well lit, but with an overpowering concentration of sweet incense smoke. It pooled in the cathedral ceiling and leaked out the windows at head level. Red light glowed from the far corner and a shrine on the wall.

"Please sit." Annie motioned to a large wooden sofa that had large red velvet cushions. "Would you like tea?"

"Uh, sure." Cale said sitting down.

Annie nodded and left. A motorcycle ripped by on the street outside. It sounded like it was in the house. In another room, the TV was blaring Chinese language and echoing strangely off the solid cement walls. Even the acoustics seemed different in this house.

Cale looked around the large room. He had lived in three different countries yet this Taiwan home was incredibly strange and foreign. Dark, with no paintings on the smoked stained walls, it reminded him of a cave.

Suddenly, without warning, Cale became acutely aware of his heartbeat. It was pounding. He took a deep breath, released clenched fists, forcibly relaxed his shoulders and turned around.

I'm sitting in the home of Helena's Grandmother in Taiwan. Cale, you're only telling her grandmother you're responsible for her granddaughter's death...

He told himself he was doing the right thing but it was not very consoling. Cale looked at the calendar on the wall. It was gilded with gold foil and red matte designs. Dragons crawled all over it. Underneath incense burned from three small reeds stuck into a bowl of sand, thick, dense and slow.

Cale had been awake for two and a half days. An incoherent six hours on the plane to Taiwan had failed to refresh his youthful body. He had been partying the entire week leading up to the bombing and everything since was now a big blur. He focused on regulating his breathing.

Queensland University had provisions for these kinds of "catastrophic" events and the rest of the year off was not just O.K., it was suggested over the phone. He was now thinking about going to Canada, as soon as possible, snow or no snow – just for a change of scenery and to visit his surrogate family. Some friends of his from school were in Thailand. He considered going to meet them for a day or two but knew they would want to talk about Helena. As tempting as it was to catch up on some sleep in a hut by the ocean, he decided it was a bad idea. Cale's Taiwan visa had two weeks. He'd decide his course then.

He had only purchased the ticket to Taiwan about thirty-six hours ago, but many of those hours had been spent thinking about what to say to Helena's grandmother. All that time spent thinking and he still had no idea what to say.

She should know about our fight. She should know about Helena's strong sense of loyalty to friends. She should know I'm responsible for her going out to the Sari Club.

Cale heard conversation outside the door. He could understand nothing. The voices stopped and Helena's grandmother, Chen Shau Dai, entered the room.

Cale found her to be a striking woman though she was well into her seventies. Helena hadn't been small, but her grandmother was three to four inches taller, with a figure that was slim. The hair was gray and pulled back into a bun.

"Cale?" The woman extended her hand to him as he stood up.

"Mrs. Chen." Cale really had no idea how he should greet her. They exchanged a gentle handshake.

"Please sit." Shao Dai motioned to the sofa he had been sitting in. She took in his presence.

So this was Helena's boyfriend. He is very handsome, but he isn't Chinese.

She had not known until the phone call that he was a foreigner. It would have been impolite to tell him to go away. Helena should never have started with him. She thought of Helena as a child when she had gone to Australia to see the family. Helena had given her such a big kiss and said, "*I love you Grandma.*" in English and everyone had been so happy. Everyone except Shao Dai. She had expected it to be said in Chinese.

"Annie will bring tea soon." Shao Dai sat down and

concentrated on understanding the boy's language.

"Thank you." It was all he could say.

"Are you tired from your trip?" Shao Dai asked wondering what kind of relative this boy would have made if events had been different.

"Yes. I haven't gotten much sleep since…" Cale found he couldn't say the word "bombing". He looked down into his lap. "Since Bali?" Those words came easier. He looked back up to her face. He saw what might have been sympathy but the whole scene was not going the way he'd envisioned.

"You have had a terrible experience." She rubbed her eyes as new tears began welling up. She'd been crying for three days and thought she might be done now. This boy was causing them again. "Helena told me you have faced many difficult times. She said you are wise for a young man."

Cale let out a sigh.

"Helena's death is the hardest experience. She was…" Shau Dai wiped tears away with ancient hands, her papery skin no longer able to hide the veins beneath.

"I loved her." Cale fought to keep his own sobs inside. He felt his emotions welling up but was simply too tired to discern among them, so they began canceling themselves out. They were all falling to the same enemy; fatigue.

It was important to get this done, and he was almost there. Shau Dai should know Helena had only been at the club because of him. She needed to know. It was the truth.

Annie brought the tea, snapping him out of his thoughts. The two ladies talked quietly in Chinese while Annie set the tray down.

Cale tried to consciously focus on the here and now but it was becoming difficult to do much more than note what he saw. Small cups. No handles. Annie poured steaming water into a small bowl full of tea leafs.

Annie gave him a small cup of the end product and said in English,

"Nice to meet you. Nice to meet you. Bye bye."

Cale stood up. He took her hand, "Very nice to meet you also." Annie bowed deeply.

Moments later, Cale was alone with Helena's grandmother.

"It was kind of you to come to Taiwan to meet me. Helena was special and it is good to meet the man who she cared about." Her voice was flat. She seemed very tired.

"Well, like I said on the phone. Helena had a wish that I meet you. It was the least I could do to honor her memory."

Helena's grandmother looked down at her tea. The tears had stopped. She had to be one hundred years old. Cale thought of how much suffering her eyes had seen.

"You are a good man." Shau Dai said and then took a sip from her cup of tea.

Cale nodded piously. He was now determined to tell her the truth about Bali. No matter how exhausted he was.

Shau Dai suddenly seemed as tired as him. "I remember when they said on the phone she was dead. So terrible. It is…difficult."

"Death is difficult." Cale choked back a little sob.

"Life. Life is so difficult." She grimaced with a regal kind of sorrow.

Cale took this as a cue, "Mrs. Chen." Her ancient

face looked into his blue eyes. "I have to tell you why Helena went to the Sari Club, where the bomb went off. It was because of me."

"I don't understand now. What are you saying?"

Maybe he was speaking too fast.

"My friend Gary, who was also killed, had asked me to do something for him and I said no. He was accused of a crime and he used me as his alibi."

"Alibi?"

"He wanted me to lie for him."

"Alibi? Police alibi?"

"He told the police he was with me. But he wasn't."

"Did he trust you?" All of sudden Shao Dai was a thousand years old.

Cale sounded uncomfortable. "Yes." Cale heard his own voice go flat.

"Was he a bad man?"

"No."

"Was he your friend?" Shao Dai looked confused.

"He was my best friend."

Shao Dai put down her teacup and seemed to collect herself. She looked very wizened.

Westerners are all the same.

"And what does this have to do with Helena going to the club?"

"She thought I should have lied for Gary. She was angry with me."

There it is. It's done.

"I'm sorry." Shao Dai was shaking her head. "I don't understand your speaking."

After a long uncomfortable pause Cale let out another deep sigh. "My friend went to the Sari Club to get away from me. Afterwards, Helena and I got into a fight because I wouldn't lie for him. She left to be with Gary and his girlfriend." Cale's voice became a whisper. "I told Helena where Gary had gone. I even told her to join him." Cale closed his eyes.

"So, what about Helena?" The voice was quiet, suspicious.

"Maybe I caused her to die." Cale shut his eyes.

"What?"

"I think I might have, caused her death." Cale said as he opened his eyes again. He was starting to sweat.

When Shao Dai finally spoke again, her voice was too low for him to hear. Something about her house made it difficult to hear voices with clarity. Cale leaned forward as he motioned that he had not heard. She tried again, "How could you come into my house?" She stood-up quickly, shaking with indignation.

"I wanted to tell the truth." Cale's voice was a whisper as he opened his eyes and looked at Helena's grandmother.

Shao Dai suddenly began to spit her words, "Before you don't tell truth? Now you tell truth? What you say to police?"

Cale gulped. It was true Cale had been processed by the police quickly, and his report had been as simple and mundane as all the others:

RELATIONSHIP TO DECEASED:
BOYFRIEND

NATIONALITY:
AMERICAN

STATEMENT:
On holiday with the deceased. Bali Nova Hotel.

It had been less than six hours after the bombing when authorities started questioning him. Her body was missing pieces and she was missing from his life.

Why is this old lady yelling at me?

"I didn't think it was any of their business…" Cale's voice trailed off.

"So why must I know?"

Cale found he had nothing to say.

"Would you lie for him now?" Her face was turning red. A strange smile began to pull the wrinkled flesh back from her teeth. She seemed to be gathering herself.

Cale stayed seated, looking up at the older woman. "I'm not sure." He let his voice trail off again.

"You are not a good man. You are bad. Ni shr bu hao! (You are bad!) Helena is better dead than with you. Sa huang de! (Liar!)" Shao Dai looked into Cale's stricken face. "Go! Bad man. Leave! Go home."

Cale stood up, a little dizzy.

What home?

The ghosts of his parents waited in Texas, the ghost of his late teens in Canada and he had three new ghosts waiting for him in Australia.

Helena's Grandmother began to cough. Tears streaming down her face now. She sat down and began to rant in Chinese between fits of coughing.

"I'm sorry," Cale choked out. He walked to the door.

"Not sorry enough." She said in perfect English.

He stopped in his tracks.

Did she say that for real? Is any of this shit real? God, when is this nightmare going to end?

Cale got out of the house quickly. He heard the gate slam behind him as he ran down the narrow street. Cale looked left and right until he had to consciously acknowledge he didn't know what he was looking for. He was physically drained and now confused as hell.

He wandered out of the neighborhood of small cement houses and came to a four-lane road. Despite the overwhelming volume of traffic there were no cabs in sight. All he wanted was a ride back to his hotel. Cale walked in a stupor down the road a ways, until he came to a set of stairs leading to a bridge that crossed over the road. He began his way to the pedestrian crossing bridge in a state of psychological shock. Out in the open sun it was now becoming unbearably hot.

Cale stopped halfway across the bridge and looked down the length of the road. He followed the vanishing point of the traffic to where it met with the yellow haze floating above. His face was long and his mouth hung open. Somewhere in the back of his mind, he realized the heat was scorching. The pollution obscured his vision in all directions. The updraft from the traffic was ridiculously thick. It was like standing on top of a smoke stack.

Cale moved slowly towards the railing and gripped it as he looked around. He felt like he was on an alien planet, with alien rules. Knowing full well how exhausted he was didn't negate the fact that he had just put himself through one of the worst experiences of his life for no good reason. He couldn't believe that had gone so badly. He had to get out of the sun and pollution.

Stepping down from the bridge, Cale headed for the first shop that looked like it would have air-conditioning. The green sign out front read **HIGH FASHION COFFEE**.

CHAPTER 7

One hour later

Sylvia's petite hands prepared the tea with proprietary care. A little steam, some crockery clinks and soon the tea was steeping in front of the small group gathered around the café table.

"How long has he been sitting there?" Vesper asked Sylvia Fong. Sylvia owned High Fashion Coffee, a hub for client hook-ups. She was also a frequent customer of Escapade, Vesper's club in Taichung. Sylvia's husband spent most of his time in Shanghai running his business operations.

"About twenty minutes. He sits there looking down at the table. He doesn't speak Chinese. So sad." She giggled with wild excitement. She and the other ladies kept their conversation in English because Nick was sitting with them. They knew he could speak Chinese, but it was much more polite to speak English in front of Nick.

Vesper appraised Cale, sitting at the dark hardwood booth in the corner. Besides Cale and Vesper's entourage, the usually bustling café was almost empty. Across from Nick, Jo Jo seemed to jiggle with excitement. She was an interior decorator. She also spent time at Vesper's club.

"Very handsome. But he is very sad looking." Jo Jo laughed. "I'd pay for him what I pay for Nick and then try and make him happy." She looked at Nick out of the corner of her eye, then added playfully, "Maybe more…"

Nick looked down at the ground, smiling the polite smile. He thought to himself, "Whatever."

"The guy's an English teacher. They're everywhere. Poor bastards can't get laid at home so they come here and hope for Asian chicks to take pity." Nick said taking a sip of his tea.

Vesper raised her left eyebrow just enough for Nick to notice. She wanted more information, "I think maybe this one is different. He doesn't look like he would have woman problems." She paused and smiled slightly as she said, "Nick, why don't you go find out?" She brushed back her hair when she finished the question.

"Huh?" Nick looked at her with surprise over his cup of tea. "What are you talking about? I don't want to talk to this guy."

"I want you to." Vesper looked at Nick with steely eyes. Nick stared back.

"No."

Vesper smiled. "This is your boss talking to you now. Time is money. Nick you know this. I'm paying you now to do this, and so will Jo Jo and May. There is no choice on this. Or do you feel threatened?"

The three ladies giggled.

"Come on, Nick." Jo Jo said sweetly.

Nick looked at the ladies.

"O.K. For you, Jo Jo." Nick said looking at Vesper. "But I'm charging for this time."

Vesper licked her lips. "Certainly, Nick."

Nick walked over to the table where the guy was sitting. He took another look at the man the ladies were so hot for.

I bet he's here for a language exchange with a desperate housewife and she didn't show. The poor guy looks all broken-up.

"Hey." Nick said as he stood next to the small table across the room.

Cale was still in a daze. He sat staring at the empty half of the booth. The man's voice seemed to come from far away. Cale wasn't sure what to say, or even who was speaking. The last thing he wanted was a conversation.

"What's up?" Cale said quietly. He continued to stare at the empty place across from the table.

"This is kind of retarded, but I'm more or less being forced to meet you by those ladies over there." Nick let that sink in. When he got no response he smiled and said, "So tell me to fuck off and I'll leave you alone. I understand."

Cale looked up into Nick's face, "I mean no offense but please, fuck off." He looked back down at the table.

Nick nodded and smiled again. "Ya, well, that was unexpected. O.K., let me try this again. My name is Nick. " He extended his hand. Nick was surprised to meet a Westerner who didn't want to strike up a conversation.

They shook hands. Cale looked at him but he couldn't get Shau Dai's angry face out of his mind. Her verbal anger at him had been red hot and the burn was still fresh. Cale was starting to think he'd never been more wrong about anything in his life. He wanted to sleep. He wanted to forget. He didn't want to talk, but he still introduced himself.

"Cale."

"Cale. That's a cool name. You got a strange accent. Where you from?" Nick did his best Bronx accent on the last sentence.

"Texas Canadian. So why are you being forced to talk to me?"

"Oh you know…women, bosses, they play these little power games." Nick looked back to the three women. They were all were staring at him from across the cafe.

"I still don't get it."

"Can I sit down for a sec?" Nick wanted to get some coffee if they were going to talk.

"O.K." Cale still wasn't sure he wanted to keep talking.

"Thanks," Nick said, sitting down. "Really, Cale, some women are a royal pain in the ass, if you'll excuse the expression." He looked straight at Cale. "You don't come here often?"

Cale smiled a little. "Here? Taiwan. No. First time."

Nick blew out a small laugh, "I meant this hole-in-the-wall coffee shop. Well, you've got your admirers now. You've either got some strange luck or maybe just good timing." Nick looked over at Sylvia and made a motion for her. Sylvia got up and quickly shuffled over. He knew she wanted to meet this stranger.

Cale stayed silent and watched.

"Yes, Nick." Sylvia looked at Nick and then Cale. Slightly, she brushed her arm smiling.

"Can I get a coffee, black?" Looking over at Cale, "Get you another?"

Cale looked at his almost empty cup, "Sure. Thanks."

Sylvia nodded. Nick stopped her from leaving. "Sylvia, this is Cale."

Sylvia looked him in the eyes. "Hello." She was star-struck. Even in his dazed state Cale couldn't help but notice the fascination in her eyes.

"Hello."

She smiled and then turned, running in strange, exaggerated baby steps.

Nick followed her with his eyes. "You'd never guess that little girl makes half a mil a year as owner of this place. She acts like a real-live *Hello Kitty*. Hubby is gone all the time. She and her friends love to meet foreign guys. You live in the city?"

"I guess I'm just passing through." Cale stared at Sylvia as she interacted with the table of ladies on the other side of the room. After the past week he wasn't sure he could continue a normal conversation.

Nick grinned, "You guess?" then he laughed a little. "Is Taiwan enticing you or kicking your ass?"

"Huh?" Cale was trying hard not to yawn. He'd felt this tired once before, at a rugby tournament in high school. No sleep for days. No one had been asking him questions at the rugby tournament. No one had questioned his morals and it had hurt less.

"Ahh... I'm just saying," Nick had stopped laughing. "Maybe you were gonna stay, but now you've changed your mind. Or you were gonna go, but now you're thinking of staying."

Cale couldn't help liking the guy

Sylvia brought the coffees. She was quick and quiet. They both thanked her.

Cale looked down into the cup, "Right now Taiwan

isn't going so well for me. I was just railed at by an old woman that has me not sure…" Cale sighed, "I better drop this shit before I say something I shouldn't." He looked up at Nick, "So, you live here?"

"Ya. For over two years."

"I guess you like it." Cale was finding conversation more and more difficult. It hadn't been an hour since Helena's grandmother had made him feel like scum and turned his world upside down. What little world he'd had left.

"Except when I'm forced to meet strangers at the whim of employers." Nick said sardonically. He took a sip of coffee and took in Cale's features. The guy was a *swhy eee gur,* meaning *handsome man* in Chinese. The blue eyes with dark hair were a good look. Nick saw why Jo-Jo, Sylvia and the others were enamored. The boy was money. Nick knew why Vesper had been so adamant about some kind of contact. Didn't make her less of a bitch.

Cale looked over at the group of women. "Which one is your boss?"

"The older one. The bimbo with the bob-cut," Nick said a little cruelly. In truth, Vesper was by far the most beautiful.

"She's really very attractive."

"You can't always judge a book by its cover. She can be a real bitch"

Cale was monotone. "Quit your job." He turned to Nick who was nodding.

"I've thought about it more than once, but it all works, mostly. I guess it's a bit of a unique situation. Anyway, enough about my job."

"Where are you from? The East?"

"So I guess you can tell I'm American?"

"I told you, you're talking to a guy who was born in Texas, went to high school in Canada and until recently was finishing up college in Australia. I can tell you aren't from any of those places. That accent has East coast all over it."

"Ya, I'm your typical Bronx hoodlum, relocated to Vegas for the chance…" Nick paused. Las Vegas seemed a long time ago. "But now, I'm here. What about you?"

"Depressing story, really…and I uhmm." Cale was silent as his brow furrowed in a look of confusion. "Even as a Roman Catholic, I kind of feel like I just got body slammed by God…I don't know; one of those things you want to talk about because maybe you'd feel better, but inside something says you can't." Cale looked down at his cup of coffee.

Nick felt the bolt of friendship. He understood that this person before him needed to talk and open up. Nick decided to offer up some information about himself.

"I sort of understand where you're coming from. My whole family is in the *big house*. My two brothers, Ma and Pop; my whole family. How the fuck do I talk about it with anyone?" Nick looked Cale straight in his eyes.

Cale choked lightly, "It has to suck."

"Oh ya. Plus, well…" Nick exhaled and knew he couldn't continue to talk about his past, "Look, I've caught you at a bad time and I should leave you alone."

"It's O.K. I'm just a little tired. I've been awake for a long time." Cale sat up a little straighter. "Have you heard about the bombings? In Bali?" Cale waited for his throat to get scratchy. He waited for his foot to move.

"Sure…" Nick's voice was low. "Everyone knows

about it. Bali blew-up. Insane." Nick looked up to the T.V. in the corner, half expecting to see the story still playing. It would again at five o'clock. A woman had died from Taiwan and they were still looking for her body.

"I lost some close friends. And my girlfriend."

Nick's curiosity became empathy, a rare emotion for him.

"That's terrible. I'm sorry, man."

"Yeah, thanks." His eyes were dull and ravaged from crying, but there seemed to be no more tears left. "There's more to it than that." Cale let out a cough. "It's kind of my fault." Cale put his hand to his head. "They went out to the club to get away from me."

Nick looked at Vesper and the girls. They were distracted for the moment. He could tell none of them were watching closely. He leaned in towards Cale.

"I don't know you and I'm the type of guy who basically doesn't give a fuck about most people's problems; ask most anybody that has been around me for any period of time. But let me give you a little advice, if I might. I can imagine you're going to spend a long time going over that night in your head. Pace yourself. You don't have to do it all now."

Nick looked back up at the TV. A popular American actress stared back at him from a shampoo commercial."

"Yeah, but if I had just..." Cale drifted off.

"You can't think like that. Fate is going on all the time. Like you and I meeting today." Nick paused. He hadn't been open with another human being in a long time. "I didn't even want to meet you. Those girls forced me to come over, more or less." Nick looked over at Vesper's crowd. They all let out stiff little giggles, except for Vesper. She was staring at them intently.

He turned back to Cale, "Now that I've met you, I'm not going anywhere. I think you need to talk, my friend."

"Talking doesn't seem to work for me right now." Cale was monotone. "About an hour ago I had the grand-mother of my girlfriend tell me that I'm a bad guy and that my girl was better off dead than with me." Cale looked from Nick to the table. He was suddenly ready to jump up and get out of this place.

"Then you walked in here, met me. It's fate. She's an old lady who has lost someone she loved. It's easy to blame you. You're the whipping boy."

"You don't know what she said to me." He choked.

"Not the things you needed to hear. That's for sure." Nick took a quick glance at the ceiling, leaning in closer. He whispered, "You really went to this girl's Chinese grand-mother? What? To tell her you killed her granddaughter?"

Cale nodded.

"I mean, Cale, come on; what did you expect?" He leaned back and took a hard look at him, "Cale, you got the time to take off for the next couple of hours?"

"What do you mean?"

"What are you doing right now?"

Cale looked at the man across from him. "Right now...I'm in limbo." Cale's voice was low.

"Cool. We're going to the fucking spa." He put his palms down on the table as if to get up.

"Spa? If it's the kind for gay guys, man, I'm not gay. I told you I had a girlfriend."

Nick laughed out loud, "It's not the kind for gay

guys. It's the kind for businessmen. It'll all make sense later, don't worry."

Cale wasn't sure, "I've never gone to a spa."

"Ya, well, your fate says first time's today. It'd be a good idea for both of us."

Cale nodded. His face said he was too tired to care. But his eyes were not glazed over anymore, they were intrigued. Perhaps this was fate. Anything would be better than the introspective nightmare he was putting himself through.

"What is the spa like? Hot tubs?" Cale asked.

"The Disneyland of water. At least, the one I go to is." Nick got up, "Come on Cale. Let me introduce you to the ladies so we can get the hell out of here."

Cale got up. "Her name is Vesper?"

"Ya. She's a cocktail. Vesper is the name of a martini."

"What?"

"Guess her folks had a twisted sense of humor. Or they liked to drink a lot."

Vesper was surprised as the men approached. Nick had been a very good boy.

"Cale this is Vesper. Vesper, this is Cale."

"It's very nice to meet you, Cale."

"Vesper, Cale and I are off to the spa."

"But you have to be at work tonight; so don't call me later and tell me you can't come in." She smiled.

Nick smiled back, she knew him too well. "Vesper, baby, like you said, I'm working tonight, I understand. But right now I'm hanging with Cale. I know all about work and what I've got to do."

"O.K., but don't forget, I've got some VIPs coming in later." She knew he probably wasn't going to show. She turned her attention to Cale. "Cale, I really hope we meet again. " To Cale she sounded like a flirt.

Nick turned away, hiding a small smile.

"Thanks," Cale said quietly.

Forty minutes later, Cale found himself in a huge building that was decorated inside like a French Baroque palace. It was a multi-leveled facility that had passageways leading from desk to lockers to baths. Steam rose steadily from the first floor. Following Nick to a couch, they both sat down and took off their shoes. A woman dressed in a tight blue uniform took his shoes and he was given a key. Nick and an attendant led the way to a dressing area with tall wooden lockers. There were no benches to sit on and the attendant stood waiting. Nick was at the locker next to him pulling off his shirt silently.

Cale opened the locker to see a towel inside, nothing else. He wasn't sure but he was getting the feeling he was supposed to strip completely. A moment later, Nick confirmed this by getting out of his clothes. Cale saw Nick reach in, grab his towel and wrap it around his waist. The attendant used a key on the lock at the bottom. Nick used his key to lock the top half.

He looked over and said. "This place is pretty safe," Nick watched Cale slip out of his pants then turned and walked out of the locker area.

Nick knew Vesper was going to like this guy physically. He paused at the stairway leading down to where the pools and saunas were. Looking back to the locker area, he saw Cale coming towards him.

"Lets hit the tubs. There are a few that can hold two or three people." Nick went down the stairs as Cale followed.

"Shower first," Nick said walking over to the ten marble cubicles off the main chamber. Each cubicle had a small blue stool and the showerheads were on silver hoses.

Cale watched Nick as he threw his towel in a nearby hamper and went to the nearest shower. Turning on the water, Nick sat on the stool and started rinsing himself off.

Cale followed suit.

The plastic stool he was sitting on felt strange. He had showered in locker rooms before, but never sitting down on a cold wet stool, bare balls.

Sitting down?

Once inside the stall, he saw that it had toothpaste, shaving cream, body wash and shampoo.

"Razors and toothbrushes are around the corner," Nick said standing up. The glass separating them was frosted so Cale made out only the figure next to him. "Want me to get any for you?" Nick stepped out of the stall.

"Sure, I'll take both." Cale said. The water was hot. It felt good.

Nick came back a moment later, gave Cale razor and toothbrush, and headed back to his shower. Nick ignored the stool and with a small sigh of relief Cale decided to do the same and stood up.

"So we just... jump into the pools after this?" Cale spoke over the partition.

"You can go swimming if you like, but I'm hitting the hot tub first. I worked out hard yesterday, I'm hurting," said Nick rinsing the shampoo out of his hair.

"How many times you been here before?" Cale said put on shaving cream. The razor was blue plastic, single blade.

"Come here quite a bit. Got turned on to spas in Vegas," Nick spoke loudly to Cale, "but I like the ones in Taiwan way better."

"Why?" Cale was almost done shaving.

"Uhm… more real." Nick turned off the water. He left the shower cubicle and looked into Cale's stall.

"Don't let Vesper see you without your clothes on or she'll turn you out."

Cale turned off the water and faced Nick. He was surprisingly at ease despite his nakedness. "What do you mean?"

"Nothing I want to get into now, but take them as friendly words of advice." Nick moved away and headed towards the hot tubs. There were four. Nick went to the largest one and Cale followed. Nick got in first and sat down. Cale joined him. The water was very hot, but far from unbearable. He sat down opposite from Nick submerging himself in the bubbling water.

"What did you mean the spas here are more real?" Cale relaxed as the water rose to lap around his face. Shao Dai was still on his mind but the guilt was fading.

This is a great diversion from feeling so shitty.

"Hmmm." Nick had shut his eyes. In a sleepy, quiet voice he said, "Spas real? Real spas. Oh… I know. The spas in Vegas are beautiful and super luxurious, but they don't have the special massage going for them."

Cale's eyes got wide. "Special massage?"

"Ya. Sometimes it can be just what the doctor ordered." Nick had already decided they were having the full treatment.

"What happens?" Cale was starting to get a little nervous. He couldn't explain why.

"A great massage with a bit of sex thrown in." Nick had decided he would take number eleven. Thirty-six would do for Cale. She spoke decent English.

"I doubt I could do that right now." Cale said looking down at the churning water. He had never been with a prostitute and the present time was definitely not appropriate to see if he could.

"It's not any hardship. You don't have to do much. She is the one that knows what to do." Nick studied Cale's face. It was almost innocent and boyish. A face that could make the man a lot of money in Nick's business.

Cale glanced around him. The place was strangely deserted except for a couple attendants milling about, straightening up towels and checking the showers. They moved slowly. "I haven't ever been with someone who gets paid."

Nick's initial reaction was to give a sarcastic comment. He thought better of it, as he looked over at Cale. The guy was still a mess. Instead he said, "There is always the first time jitters and I guess it does feel a little strange. Just remember, you're a treat for her." Nick looked at his new friend. "I speak with a bit of experience."

"I guess this is your way of telling me you use prostitutes a lot." Cale looked at his fingers. They were starting to get wrinkled.

Nick stood up. "Lets go to the steam room. Good for the chest."

Cale got up and followed Nick again. As they walked, Cale saw two attendants stare at him. It looked like they had their eyes centered on his crotch.

"Why are those guys looking at our dicks?" Cale asked as they entered the opaque steam room.

"Because we're foreigners and they think we all have big cocks."

"Doesn't it bother you?"

"I have blond hair. People look at me all the time. It's the same thing with having a Western cock. Chinese want to look."

They sat down on the benches.

"Yeah, but they'd get knocked out if we were back home."

Nick looked down at the wet floor of the steam room. He took a deep breath in and let it out again with a compressed hiss.

"Cale you aren't back home, are you?" The steam continued to hiss in the background.

"No, but it's still gay to me."

"Cale most of the men who come here are businessmen or mafia types. The mafia runs this place. So trust me, nobody is looking at your cock with any more interest than your biceps or hair color. Your cock exists. You aren't wearing clothes so it's out for everyone to see. If you are that bothered, wear a towel, you're a foreigner, they will accept it."

Cale shook his head. The steam was thick and the room hot. He could barely see Nick who was sitting next to him. "Guess I'm a bit of a redneck, but I don't like it."

"Cale when in Rome, you do as the Romans.. Don't

expect other people to bend to your way of thinking. No one is saying you have to stare back. The test is how well you deal with it."

Cale breathed in. Running into this guy was a good thing. Talking to Nick was cauterizing some of his wounds. The spa was forcibly relaxing muscles in his legs and back that had become rigid after days without sleep.

"So this massage; you're going to have it?"

"We are both going to have it." Nick looked down at his feet.

"I don't want to." He really didn't.

"Cale do me a favor. Go to the little private room; get a massage; if you don't want more, no problem. Price is the same and it's my treat."

"Why?"

Nick sighed and looked up. He thought about how to answer. "You really want to hear the reasoning?"

"You bet." Cale breathed in deep. Heat from the steam was taking over his lungs. It felt great.

Nick exhaled long and loud. He wasn't going to go into his life story so he said, "Cale I know you don't have to trust me after meeting me for only an hour, but after what you told me, this probably is a start in the right direction."

"By being with a whore?"

"Ya, by being with a whore," Nick said in a lower voice, "I'm not trying to tell you to forget the past, death is unavoidable, but you are alive, man."

Cale took in what Nick was saying. He changed the subject. "Can we go to a another pool, not hot or too cold?"

"Sure. There is no hurry. For anything." Nick got up. Both walked out as a blast of steam began filling the chamber with fresh heat. They ended up at a long lap pool with swirling waters.

Both men stayed silent in the water. It was Cale who broke the silence.

"This place is pretty cool. Is it really run by the mafia?" Cale looked around at the small waterfall cascading down into the next pool over.

"Well, let's just say, it is run by people who know people, who know mafia. They have to be connected to get their ...business license, sort of."

"How do you mean?"

"Cale you are in a culture that is all about who you know and what can be done because of favors and kindness." Nick smiled a little.

"Corruption, huh?"

"That's everywhere. Not just here."

"Yeah, but now you have exploited women who are trapped by their circumstances."

"There are lots of looks in this world Cale and this isn't some Texas whorehouse. This place doesn't use underage, mistreated prostitutes. These ladies are here for their own reasons and some of them are happy to be here. It's a job."

"I still don't like the idea of a job that abuses women that aren't from the first world."

"Jesus, Cale. Look around you. This country is emerging just fine. As far as prostitution goes, I'd say the U.S. is way worse. I don't want to get into a stat war, but before you accuse me of contributing to the downfall of this society, take a hard look at the world around you." Nick paused and said in a lower, scratchy voice, "You of all people should know bad exists on this planet. There's good, bad and lots and lots of grey."

"Yeah, but prostitution…"

"O.K., O.K. So go back to the original plan. Have the massage, no sex."

"I could use the massage. Not the prostitute."

"Cale, I can certainly send you to one of those men over there that give massages if you want. You can bet your ass they won't try and have sex with you." Nick squinted at the sign over the small booth in the corner. "Those guys are totally professional. But trust me, the women are way better. Even without the sex. They have a softer touch and I think you need it right now."

Cale glanced over at the small room with two customers inside laying face down on massage tables. A grey haired man was rubbing one of their backs vigorously, but distractedly as he watched the television mounted in the corner of the room.

"I don't know."

"I dare you to be strong."

"Huh?" Cale felt a little anger rising.

"I dare you to be strong and face a preset judgment you have without any knowledge to back it up."

Cale shook his head. "Where did that come from?" Just listening to this man was a challenge. He seemed to have all the angles on Taiwan, all the angles on life as well. Cale was too tired to think of rebuttals and there was no harm in listening.

"Be burly. It's a small step towards putting the past behind you. I really believe that." Nick leveled a stare at him.

Cale looked down at the bubbling water. "O.K. I'll have the massage with the woman. But really, I don't want sex."

Nick smiled, "Famous last words." He thought. A little red from the heat, he stood up and said, "Cool, let's go."

Together they headed towards the dressing area. Stacks of clean boxer shorts and cotton robes were at the guest's disposal. A man in front of Cale began to pull on a pair of spa issue boxers.

Cale laughed a little as he slid into a pair of shorts marked LARGE. "I thought I was going to have to walk around naked." He struggled with the waistline, "These seem a little small for a large."

Nick smiled and nodded "Welcome to Taiwan, one size fits all."

After they dressed, Nick led Cale to a hallway leading to a dining area. Cale could smell food somewhere and there were at least a dozen men lounging in high-backed cushion chairs watching T.V. They were all wearing the same boxers and robes.

At the end of the hallway, a wizened old man stopped them. His tanned skin folded comfortably into a large smile, "You want special massage?" *ma sa gee*.

"Women yow massage. Wo yow shau jai shr yi. Wude hao pungyo yow shau jai san shr leo." ("We'd both like a massage. I'll have number eleven. My friend would like number 36.")

Although the old man's seasoned smile faded a bit as Nick spoke, something in the timeworn features relaxed, signifying some level of respect.

Cale observed the exchange as though it was a foreign film. Unlike French or Spanish, he understood absolutely nothing except for the exaggerated 'massage'. He watched the old man intently as his leathery hand rose to knock on the wood paneled wall behind him. A moment later the panel opened by remote leading to another hallway. Branching off into a warren of smaller tributaries, the secret part of the complex seemed just as large as the rest of it.

"I picked out a number for you." Nick said as the three moved along the plush carpet of the main passageway.

"Number?"

"The girls don't have names. Only numbers. So if you find someone you like and you come here a few times, you ask for the girl by number."

"So… you've used the woman who is giving me my massage?" Cale stopped and looked at Nick.

"Cale you're only getting a massage. I picked her because she speaks a bit of English. You got to be able to communicate with your masseuse."

Cale nodded. He was sleep deprived, he knew from experience it made him over think a little. He was only getting a massage. It didn't really matter what Nick had done with the woman in the past.

"These ladies really give a good massage?"

"Most of the time. If you don't like it, get up, go chill-out and watch some T.V. downstairs. You can do whatever you want." Nick patted Cale's shoulder.

"Enjoy."

The old man opened the door to a small room lit

by a single red bulb in the corner. A massage table in the middle of the room was the only piece of furniture. There was a shower enclosure in the back.

"O.K., I'll see you in about an hour, downstairs." Nick said as Cale entered the room. The old man closed the door shutting out the dim light from the hallway. Chinese muzak played on a P.A. somewhere.

Cale sat down on the massage table. He breathed deep looking up at the clock, prominently placed in the middle of the wall. Three P.M.

There was a slight mildew smell but everything seemed clean. He began to realize his whole body was ragged with fatigue. The baths proved that. The heat had forcibly relaxed his muscles and now he felt incredibly sleepy. His mind was a blank as he stared at the wallpaper around the clock. The muzak droned in the background.

Suddenly, questions began to flood his mind.

How had this happened? How have I found myself sitting in a Taiwanese whorehouse at three in the afternoon on a Sunday? This guy Nick is helping me deal with Helena's death in his own way. But wouldn't Helena be disgusted he was here? What would his parents think about him if they were alive?

He held back tears that were threatening to return now.

The small red pattern made the room seem darker than it was. The faux blue leather of the table caught the weak red light coming from a small armoire in the corner.

There was a knock at the door. A petite, attractive woman in a sexy, tight fitting blue dress entered.

"Hello," she said softly. She was smiling broadly.

"Hi." Cale was nervous. This woman was much

more attractive than what he'd expected.

She said coming closer. "Yow shr."

"What?"

"Key." She smiled again. She could tell he was new. She was going to take care of him. Her perfume sweetened the room.

"Oh, here," Cale showed the key which was on his wrist.

"Thank you." She wrote his number down on a pad. Abruptly, she turned and left the room.

Cale had never felt this exhausted and sitting in this tiny dark room was not very sexy at all. The knock came again, and before he could answer, the same woman opened the door, bringing her smell and a little more light back into the room. This time she was carrying a plastic box with bottles of oil and hot towels. She shut the door behind her. The room was again bathed in a sedentary darkness.

She put down the basket at the armoire. Even in the low light, Cale could make out the delicate features of her face. The hooded eyes looked at him.

"Please put your robe there." She pointed to a hook on the wall across from the bed.

Cale took off the robe. He was now clad only in the cotton boxers. Number 36 went to a drawer and pulled out a large white towel. She looked back at him. "Please, shorts too." Her friendly business-like manner lent her a subtle authority that made it a reasonable request.

Cale gulped a little and without hesitating further, slipped out of the trunks. He put the shorts on the hook and faced her.

"Please lay down. Stomach. Stomach." She patted

the table that she had covered with a fresh sheet. Cale lay face down on the massage table. The towel was draped over his buttocks.

"O.K., this is alright," he told himself.

Hot oil went down the middle of his back.

"You are friend of Nick." She whispered in his ear.

"Yeah," Cale said. Hands were now spreading the oil on his back and shoulders. Cale's eyes were shut. He was getting sleepy fast.

"You have a nice body. Strong. Relax. You relax now." She started to knead his shoulders with her palms.

"Thanks." Cale's voice was almost a whisper. It felt good to have the hands on him. His troubles were still there, but they were buried deep in a burst of endorphins released by the massage. It felt good to let someone touch him.

"You are American, like Nick?" Her hands had gone to his biceps. It felt great.

Cale nodded. He could smell her perfume as she went up and down his arms.

"You are very, very handsome." The voice purred in his ear. She was so close. It helped relax him even further. The physical stress was leaking out of him now.

Tension evaporated. Her touch was magic. The aromatic hot oil was seeping into his skin made soft by the baths. Her hands went to his legs. She started with his ankles, kneading forcefully. Oil went onto his calves as she worked over those muscles with surprising force and dexterity. Minutes of silence passed as she went to work on his hamstrings. The towel was shifted higher, past his buttocks as she pushed on the upper legs and gluteus maximus.

Despite all his initial resistance to the idea, he found

himself becoming aroused. At this point he was too tired to care. He could feel the blood rushing and coursing through his body to his penis. The hands were now clutching and kneading his ass muscles. The towel was gone. He was naked. She roamed her scented touch over his exposed body, from time to time brushing against his flesh with her breasts. "Was she naked, too?" he questioned in silence.

As she rubbed, her hands edged towards his scrotum in slow concentric circles. He was about to tell her to stop, but it didn't really make sense, she hadn't done anything. His body overruled him. For the first time since the bombing he was not focused on death.

"Up."

"Huh?" Cale wasn't sure what she meant. Being face down, he opened his eyes. His vision was blurry as though he'd been asleep for hours.

"Up on your hands and knees." She moved around him, gently manipulating him into position so he was on all fours. His buttocks were raised a little too high for comfort. He caught brief glimpses of her naked form as she moved around him.

How had she gotten her dress off?

She came to his side, intentionally brushing her tight body against him. The breasts were small with cocoa pink nipples. As Cale watched, his hairline resting on the table between his elbows, she got more oil, splashed it on his back, then went behind him and got on the table herself, kneeling behind him. She rubbed oil on his back and in between his legs, gently massaging his testicles.

Cale was fully hard. She was now gently touching everything in the groin area. The primal part of his brain was taking over, shutting down thought processes. He could only observe now. And relax. He was supposed to relax. There was going to be no asking her to stop. He didn't even know how to anyway. More oil was poured into the cleft of his buttocks. With one hand she lightly rubbed his sternum, testicles and rectum. The other hand massaged his erection with expert ability.

"You're so big. Beautiful. Big." she whispered. "Please let me touch it more." She took his hard-on in both hands and he felt her slide on a condom. Number 36 rolled him onto his back.

Cale complied in silence. Within moments she was riding him, up and down, moaning, "You are a superman."

His hands reached instinctively for her breasts.

"Ahhhh… Hhhhd… Ahhh. You are so big." The woman bent down and pressed her breasts into his hands.

Cale thrust upwards.

"Ahhh…" She moaned and started to speak Chinese. "Bao Chein. Bao Chien." (I am so sorry.)

Cale had no idea what she was saying. He thrust deep again. Her hair draped his face. Sensation filled his mind. It was so much better than the questions that had been there before.

"Ahh… Oh… Oh… No…" the woman grew rigid as she let out a series of loud screams. Her hair disappeared as she flung her head back in apparent ecstasy.

Cale exploded into his condom.

She gripped his shoulders as she tried to extend his climax with her own contractions.

"You are great lover," she said, a little out of breath as she lifted herself off carefully. "Very great."

Cale sighed. He was drained. Some kind of critical mass had been reached. "Thanks. You too."

"We still have fifteen minutes. Do you want shower?" She pulled off the condom and started to wipe him with a cotton towel. He propped himself up on his elbows and watched as she wiped carefully around the sensitive tip. When she was done she looked down at him, sizing him up, taking time to look over his body.

"What is it?" He asked hoarsely.

She removed the towel and took him in her hands, stroking him up and down.

"I want this. I want more."

Cale shut his eyes as she applied herself to his returning hard on.

"O.K.," he thought passively to himself. "There is a time and place for paid sex and this it." He closed his eyes and felt another condom being put on. A moment later, he was lost again in a world comprised completely of sexual response.

Thirty minutes later, clean and a bit dazed, Cale was escorted downstairs to the lounge. He searched the overstuffed chairs and found Nick sitting alone, smoking a cigarette.

Nick smiled as Cale approached and sat down across from him. Cale smiled sheepishly back at him and looked down at his left foot. It was tapping the carpet.

"Hope it was a good massage." Nick took a deep drag off his cigarette and exhaled. There was a plastic cigarette dispenser on the table.

"Yeah, it was good." Cale let out a mischievous grin.

"Did she touch anything she shouldn't have?" Nick

put out his cigarette. "The ladies aren't shy about messing around with the no-no spot."

Cale sat down opposite Nick and got himself comfortable in the leather lounge chair. "What the hell is a no-no spot?"

"That's what Vesper calls assholes and areas good girls don't talk about." Nick rubbed his nose and made eye contact with Cale. He laughed a little.

"Is this what all prostitutes do?"

"What do you mean?"

"I was a little shocked at all the attention she gave my ass." Cale repeated. "Do all prostitutes do that?"

Nick looked down. "These ladies over here know a lot about sex. The ass is part of the playing field. No part of the body is off limits." Nick laughed. "So... can I assume you are happy with whatever happened behind those closed doors?"

Cale shook his head. "I confess. I had sex and it was great." He looked at the box containing the cigarettes. "I've never had a girl touch my ass so much."

Nick lit another cigarette and said, "When you are in the sex industry, you have to know every way to give a client pleasure. The women over here concentrate on the ass because most of their customers like it. I guess it's a Chinese thing."

"Yeah, O.K.," Cale gave out a little laugh. "I totally understand why you wanted me to come. I've got to say thanks."

Nick felt the warmth of friendship growing between them. It had been a long time since he'd felt this. Cale had taken Nick's advice and seemed to have benefited. Nick was feeling comfortable enough to open up a small amount about his life in Taiwan.

"I know more than I should about how the sex trade works in this country."

"Huh?" Cale didn't get what Nick was saying.

"Let's go back to the pools. I want one more soak before calling it a day. I'll explain what I mean there."

Cale nodded and got up with Nick. They walked back to the pools in silence. As Nick got to the disrobing area and started to strip down he said, "I have a job that uses this." He pointed at his boxer shorts.

"What do you mean?"

"I'll spill my guts over at the Jacuzzi pool." Nick tossed his shorts into a hamper and turned towards the first pool again.

Three minutes later, Cale was waiting for Nick to make some sense. He could feel endorphins repairing his body.

"Uhm… Short version. You are looking at a Friday Boy."

"And that is?"

"Women pay to go to bed with me. I'm sort of an escort but it is a bit different than back in the States." Nick watched as Cale's eyebrows were pulled back like curtains.

"You're fucking joking." Cale shook his head a little.

"No, I'm not." Nick splashed his face. "Vesper is my boss and supervisor."

"Supervisor of what, exactly?" Cale couldn't believe this. He was intrigued.

"Short story is she recruited me back in Vegas where I was a dancer." Nick sat up straighter. "I'm a pretty good dancer, but I got this rebel streak which gets me in trouble."

"What sort of trouble?"

"Usually job trouble." Nick laughed. "I'm a little too inclined to improvise versus being totally choreographed." Nick sighed. "Very frustrating for all concerned, but it's my nature."

"You met Vesper in Vegas?"

"Ya. She saw me dancing. Guess I forgot to mention she owns a lot of clubs for women."

Cale laughed a little. "You're a real American gigolo."

"Laugh, but I've done pretty well the past couple years."

"If it's working out for you that's great. I don't think I could ever do that shit for money."

"Definitely not for the average bear." Nick splashed his face again.

"Are you her only Westerner?"

"Ya. A couple fellas asked me to give them an in with Vesper but… well, it's not easy." Nick saw he had Cale's attention. "You gotta have really good looks and then Vesper has to be attracted to you as a marketable property."

"Business is business."

"Vesper is all business, all the time." Nick continued to look at Cale as he said the next words, "The only other Western guy she's shown any interest in is sitting across from me now."

Cale looked back at Nick. "Me!"

"Yep. That was why I was pissed off when we first met. I'm not exactly the recruiting officer type."

"Are you recruiting me now?"

Cale kept his eyes on Nick.

"No. Life just up and slapped the shit out of you, and I'm trying to help."

"It's much appreciated." Cale said. He smiled, but now he was not so sure of Nick's motives. It was as if the guy was reading his mind.

"Look, I'm not a person a lot of people trust because I come across like I'm only looking out for myself. It's a nice change when I can do something without thought of gain."

"No gain with me?" Cale wasn't convinced.

Nick looked down. "Sure, if I've made a friend today, there is some gain." In a lower tone he said, "Don't have many friends in Taiwan."

Cale thought to himself, "What an unlikely lifesaver fate had thrown his way; a male prostitute."

"You think I should sign up?" Cale said, not very seriously.

"That is your choice man. The job is probably there; but this whole spa thing… well… it's the way I figured I could make you feel better." Nick looked up at Cale.

"Well it worked." Cale smiled.

"As for Vesper and what she has planned for you, you don't have to even consider it, just look at it as a compliment." Nick looked back up into Cale's eyes and said, "It's like the massage; you can stop anytime you want."

Cale smiled. Nick had a sense of humor. He liked that in a friend.

"Yeah, I was very stoic."

"I bet. When did you give in? Hot oil on the balls?" He laughed.

"I threw in the towel when she took away my towel."

Cale sat back and shut his eyes.

"Cale, we really don't know each other and this whole recruitment thing is…well…maybe it doesn't put you and me on the best footing." Nick looked at Cale's eyelids. He continued, "I really am sorry about you losing so many people you cared about in such a bullshit way."

Cale kept his eyes shut as he spoke softly, "Those are good words to hear right now." A rush of tears felt seconds away.

"Then I'm glad I'm saying them."

"What's next? You going to work?" Cale asked as he got control. His voice was becoming faint. Sleep was what he needed.

"Nah, let's go out and get a little drunk. Let me show you Taichung." Nick grinned.

"Didn't I hear Vesper say… something about VIPs?"

"Don't worry about that. Vesper will be fine. She knows me and I know her. She's not going to be happy, but she knew when I walked out the door, I wasn't coming in tonight." Nick rubbed some water off his cheek as he said the last words.

"Sounds like you have it all figured." Cale laughed as he woke up just a little. He was feeling good. Even better, there was little guilt about the sex he'd just had.

"Sometimes the hardest part about a job is letting people think they're in control."

They both laughed out loud again.

Cale let out a big yawn. "I am beat. I'd give anything for a little sleep."

"You can do that. There are some beds for you to crash on."

"There are?"

"Ya. Why don't you go crash for a few hours."

"What are you going to do?"

"Well, I think I might try another number." Nick gave Cale a wicked smile.

Cale laughed again at his new friend.

CHAPTER 8

"I know you were bar hopping last night instead of being here." Vesper poured water in the red clay teapot. The water had steam rising.

"You're the one who wanted me to become buddies." Nick lit a cigarette.

Vesper was agitated. Nick was right, but definitely not playing by her rules.

"What's he like?"

"I like him. He's cool." Nick exhaled a strong stream of smoke.

"Did you explain things?"

"He knows."

"What sort of body does he have?" Vesper knew the answer but wanted to hear what Nick had to say.

"Athletic. I imagine most of your ladies aren't going to kick him out of bed for eating crackers." Nick smiled sweetly at her.

"What?" Even Vesper's tone was perplexed. She hated when Nick used sentences she couldn't understand.

"It means yes, he's well built." Nick was getting tired and annoyed with this line of questioning.

Vesper smiled. "Is his equipment as good as yours?"

Nick shook his head. "Nope he's got a little dick." Then he gave her a wicked grin.

"Really?" She knew better. The woman Cale had been with at the spa had already told her about him. She wondered if Nick was jealous.

"Vesper, I did what you asked. Get off my back."

"You are impossible." Vesper brushed back her hair. Her eyes were serious.

"No I'm not. Cale coming on board is your pet project, not mine. I'm not gonna start giving you cock measurements because you can't do your own research."

"Nick, don't start this again."

"Start what again?" Nick's anger registered in his voice.

"You know who is going to win. Telling me big, small, average isn't really such a big deal."

"Vesper, let's have a little understanding here." Nick cleared his throat. "After two years, I know how to buy a plane ticket and I'm not scared to leave."

"Are you making a threat?" growled Vesper.

"I think we are at a crossroads." Nick's eyes were cold steel. "You order me around and treat me like I'm some toy. This is business and business demands a certain amount of respect. I make money and you make money." Nick looked Vesper straight in the eyes and said, "Can't say you've been over generous in the respect department lately."

"That's funny, I see it the other way around."

"Whatever, Vesper." Nick looked away.

She took a deep breath. This anger would not serve

her. She could not afford to lose Nick over such a stupid fight.

"Nick, I'm sorry we both are feeling unhappy. Maybe I am…well; you don't have to get me any more information on Cale. Just maybe help me meet him."

"He might not be interested. I already told you, he's got a lot on his mind." Nick had made sure to leave out specifics.

"I understand. But he might be receptive to me." Vesper licked her lips.

Nick smiled sensing a small victory.

"Vesper baby, every man is receptive to you."

Vesper smiled and tilted her head. Then she playfully slapped him on the right side of his face. This was the Nick she liked.

Nick laughed as he rubbed his tingling cheek. All was well between them again.

(Six Days Later)

"Thank you for coming Cale." Vesper got up from her stool at the elegant bar. Situated on the thirty-fifth floor, the views of the city were commanding.

Cale nodded, took her extended hand, lightly shook it and said politely, "It was kind of you to invite me."

Vesper sat down back in her stool, as did Cale.

"What would you like?" Vesper asked as the attractive, young, female bartender came over.

"Crown on the rocks." Cale told her seeing a bottle of Crown Royal on the back bar. Vesper translated.

A minute later his drink was in front of him.

"Nick and you seem to get along well." Vesper looked down at her glass. "He's been taking off a lot of time from work this week to show you around." If Cale didn't come to work for her, she was not going to be pleased over Nick's absence. Two very important women left one night when they found out he was not available.

"Maybe he needed a small break from work and I happened to come around at the right time." After taking a sip from his drink, Cale said in a lower voice. "No doubt, he has been very cool to me." He didn't know how to take this meeting. Nick was working tonight. He had told Cale to talk with Vesper so he could get some peace from her nagging. Reluctantly, Cale had agreed to meet this evening.

"I almost find it hard to believe someone has made Nick human. He is usually so unreachable." Vesper sipped on a glass of white wine.

"You know, I think a boss isn't going to appreciate the qualities in a individual if it is always about how much money they can make. There is no looking at the person's core."

Vesper looked up. It wasn't what she expected to hear. She took it in. He wasn't stupid or scared to speak his mind. "You could be right Cale." Vesper said in a low voice. "Nick is special to me. I brought him to Taiwan for several reasons. Some have worked out and some have not." Vesper looked directly into Cale's face. "But as you probably know, Cale business is about profit. Emotions play very little in business."

"What are you selling, if you aren't selling emotions?"

"I don't understand."

Vesper looked at him questioningly.

"Why do ladies come to you and buy men like Nick?"

"They are buying a good time."

"Yeah, plus I bet a lot more."

"I don't understand."

"A good time is one thing. Sex is another. At some point, the seller is saying and doing the right things to make some client happy and return. That doesn't mean there is any sincerity involved."

"You are over thinking." Vesper thought silently, "This young man is not only handsome but smart. Very smart."

"No I'm not. You are dealing with human emotions, yet you are pretending it doesn't happen. You are ignoring what is damaging and beneficial." Cale took a sip of his drink. He wasn't really sure if this woman was going to listen much more. Her face was impassive, but her brown eyes had fire in them.

"I'm glad to hear the word beneficial." Vesper's anger stirred deep down inside. Cale was testing her patience. Nick had prepared him for this moment.

"I said before, it's about emotions." Cale took another sip of his drink.

"Were you emotional at the spa?" Vesper looked into Cale's eyes.

Cale didn't flinch. Nick had warned him that Vesper would know about the encounter at the spa. "Sure. "

"Why?"

"Sorry. Not open for discussion." Cale kept eye contact.

Vesper made her voice gentle. "Cale lets try and see

if we can find some common ground."

Cale stayed silent, but nodded.

"I find you to have a face that is quite pleasing to look at." Vesper tried to make her voice sound nice.

"Thank you."

She looked at his chest. He looked at her eyes.

"Let's start this way. I don't think you are worried about money." She said, looking up suddenly.

Cale nodded again. "Money isn't an issue in my life."

"So I'm going to offer you an opportunity to learn about yourself and others."

Cale interrupted. "But it is about selling me."

"True, but I think you need a shelter for the time being. A job that affords you freedom."

"Like the freedom you give Nick?"

"Nick needs money."

"So I'll be selling myself because why…?"

"To redeem yourself."

"Huh?"

"I'm going to speak honest. O.K.?"

"O.K."

"I know quite a lot about you from different sources. For one thing I know you are good in bed and that you can give pleasure to a woman. That source is obvious." She paused and saw no reaction. Vesper continued. "I know your ticket is extendable, but you're scheduled to leave in five days to Canada."

"How do you know that? Nobody knows. I haven't told anyone my departure date. Not even Nick."

"I'm being honest with you Cale. I found out a lot. Nick has told me very little but when I seek information, I have many places I can go."

"Keep talking."

"I know your family was killed about fifteen years ago. I'm sorry about that." Vesper saw he did blink this time. "Today I learned about your girlfriend. Again I'm so sorry. A terrible way to go."

"You do know a lot." Cale's voice was quiet.

"I think we could be good for each other."

"Me fucking for money and you get some of the action, right?" Those were the words Nick used describing Vesper's business. Cale's tone was hard but even. He didn't like her knowing so much about his past.

"You sound like Nick." Vesper said with a sigh.

"He would be the guy who knows, don't you think?"

"No. Nick sees life one way. You can see it another way."

"I don't have what it takes to be a Friday Boy."

"There are different reasons men come to work for me."

"What do you mean?"

"It is not always about money. Even Nick. I think he came here for..." She stopped herself. Vesper decided it wasn't the right time to mention her thoughts on Nick. "Cale, I have only ever asked one other Western man to work for me."

"Nick told me that."

"I hope you take it as a compliment."

"I do, but I wouldn't even know how to start to take money from a woman for sex." Cale took a sip of his whiskey.

"I'll show you how." Vesper moved closer. Her voice

was lowered, "I'll pay you fifty thousand NT an hour, over thirteen hundred U.S. dollars, for your time. I've already booked a suite." Vesper looked at him like she had just suggested tea for two.

She was offering a fortune. He found himself asking, "You're testing me out?"

"No. You are testing me out."

Cale smiled. This was crazy. He didn't know why, but he was thinking of saying yes just to spite her.

"O.K.?" Vesper asked quietly.

Cale threw out one more attempt at resistance. "I don't think you get the message, Vesper. Sex with you would be wrong." He wanted to believe his words.

Vesper took his hand and placed it on her bare leg. "I want you in me. You are making me ready to beg."

"What does she really want?" Cale thought to himself. He was going to be out of this country in a week. "I'll do it for a hundred thousand NT an hour." Cale downed the last of his drink.

Vesper beamed at her victory.

"Deal." As she paid the bill Vesper turned to him, "I hope I'm getting at least four hours."

Cale was a bit dazed as he stood up from the bar and looked at her saying, "You may only be getting ten minutes if I change my mind."

"Cale, I'll take whatever you give me." She said cryptically as she took his hand. They walked to the elevator together.

Vesper turned on the lights. It revealed a well-appointed hotel suite overlooking the city with a forty-story view.

Cale walked in feeling tense. He asked himself several times silently, "Why he was here?"

Vesper went to the bathroom telling him, "I'm going to freshen up."

Cale nodded and looked out at the sparkling lights of this alien city through the immense window that took up the entire wall. Helena wasn't dead two weeks and he was getting ready to have sex with woman number two.

"You know, I don't think this is a good idea," Cale said watching Vesper put her purse down on the small desk in the corner of the room. "I sound like a broken record." he thought silently.

"What?" Vesper turned around to look at him.

"I'm being stupid." Cale took a deep breath.

"Or maybe being smart." Vesper came closer to where he was standing.

Cale was confused. This certainly wasn't what he expected to hear.

"You're facing the unknown right now. It can cause a little fear." Vesper went over to the bed and sat down. Cale stayed where he was. Close to the door.

"Fear and smart work together, I guess," Cale said out loud, but inside he told himself, "No matter what, tonight you have met one interesting lady."

"Adrenaline (She pronounced it adrene-o-lene) is one of the most powerful substances our body produces. Very powerful."

"So I'm afraid?" Cale questioned.

"It would be very natural." Vesper leaned back on the bed.

Cale took a step forward, "Why?"

She licked her lips. "I can see you want to look inside."

"Inside?" Cale came over and sat down on the bed next to her.

"Tear down all you have been taught and piece it back together. Start fresh. Most people are too scared. They end up denying so much."

"I'm sitting next to you aren't I? You're happy now."

Vesper laughed. "Yes, I am."

She took his hand. Cale let her rub his fingers. "Do you have sex with all your perspective employees?"

"That is a secret."

Cale smiled, "Should I say this is a recruitment drive or a training session?" He was getting more interested about Vesper's intentions, but he still felt he should leave.

Vesper let go of Cale's hand and slid her's over his chest. Her nails pushed the fabric of his shirt next to his skin.

"Neither." She lightly kissed his cheek.

His fear was gone and he found himself responding to her attention.

"Let's take a shower first." Vesper pulled back.

Cale grabbed her arms and stopped her from getting up. "No. It's now or never."

Thirty minutes later, Vesper was planted on top of Cale, facing him, meeting his thrusts; sweat dripping from her neck to the cleft of her breasts. His hands were on her hips, squeezing tight so as not to slip off.

Vesper was panting. This was a man who knew how to use the equipment nature gave him. She contracted her muscles to make his thrusts more intense. Vesper saw his eyes were shut.

"Don't shut your eyes Cale." She could barely talk, but she had her eyes open.

Cale opened his but intentionally avoided her gaze. Instead he slowly looked at the chest above him. Dangling off her exquisite breasts was a gold locket. Heart shaped.

He stopped his thrusting and took the locket in his hand.

Vesper, still mounted, saw him take the gold heart between his thumb and fingers.

"Where did you get this?" Cale said quietly looking into her eyes.

"From someone long ago" Vesper whispered.

The past crept into both their minds.

CHAPTER 9

Hanna, Alberta
Ten Years Earlier

"I thought I'd find you here."

Cale looked up from the vista that was before him. It was his cousin Jace.

"I didn't know you were getting back today. Aunt Katy said you weren't coming in until late tomorrow." Cale was sitting on an outcrop of rocks that overlooked a canyon. There was a reservoir in the distance with a couple buildings, but besides those structures, there was little sign of mankind. The wind was blowing strongly.

"Got an earlier flight. Mind if I join you?"

"Feel free, this was your spot before it was mine."

"Yeah, I have to admit, there are plenty of times that I miss it."

"Toronto losing its appeal?"

"Nah. I'm not a small town boy. I don't miss Hanna very much. I do miss being able to walk a mile from our house and being in the middle of nowhere and sorting out my thoughts. Although, I forgot how many dogs bark from behind their fences as you walk down the street to get to this trail. Hanna is definitely not a cat town."

The wind blew stronger.

There was silence between the two.

"So happy birthday, one day late. Turning seventeen is a big deal."

Cale nodded. "Yeah, I guess so."

"I heard you went out with the Rothby twins last night."

Cale let out a sigh. "Well, you know, rite of passage, got to get drunk and fuck some bimbo."

"Who was the lucky lady?"

"Diane Foxton."

"Is that Foxy Roxy's little sister?"

"Yeah."

"Does she have the same big tits?" Jace was six years older than Cale. He had left home before Cale came to live with the Wilhoute family. Jace, like Cale, was an only child. When Cale came to live in Canada, Jace had just graduated college and been home for a couple of months. Jace took the sad teenager under his wing and treated him like a kid brother. He was a good friend and Cale had missed him when he went to work in Toronto. Jace was a film editor and work was only there or Vancouver. He was also a devotee to different martial arts and an avid hunter. Bow weaponry was his specialty.

"She has big tits." Cale looked over and smiled.

There was silence again as both looked out onto the vast landscape.

"I heard today there was a little scene with the folks."

"Yeah, I was a jerk. I owe Aunt Katy an apology. I don't know why I made such a big deal of it."

"Well, it could be this is your birthday and you miss your folks."

Cale nodded as he continued to look out at the endless prairie and canyon lands. "I shouldn't have yelled."

"No, you probably shouldn't have. They love you bro. But that locket is yours, not Mom's. She knows that. I think she wears it to remind her of her little sister. But she feels bad."

"I'm such an asshole."

"I don't know how I would handle my folks being gone. They are my stability."

"They've been really good to me."

"Yeah, but let's face it, you hardly knew each other before this shit happened. They love you, but it isn't the same as your parent's love. I know."

Cale looked over at Jace. He was a fairer, older version of Cale. "I miss my folks so bad Jace."

"I'm sure you do."

Cale choked a little. Tears were forming. "I'm almost ready to cry. I don't know why seeing the locket on Aunt Katy made me go crazy. I've seen her wear it before."

"Yeah, but you may be attached to things we don't understand. That locket might be one of them."

"My mother wore it all the time."

"That is what my Mom said. She also said it's yours now." Jace stood up and reached into his pocket. He pulled out the locket that had made Cale go crazy today. He sat back down and held out the gold jewelry.

"Mom has only been wearing it because she didn't want it to go into a box or something. You know who gave it to your mother, don't you?"

Cale was at a loss. He looked at the shiny locket that was reflecting the bright sun. He could only shake his head.

"My mom did. On your mother's eighteenth birthday. She told your mother to use it and put the picture of the man she loved inside."

Cale choked. He felt terrible.

Why was this happening?

Jace put his arm around his cousin. "Hey, it was a misunderstanding."

Cale whispered, "I said some bad things. I called her a thief and a grave robber. I guess you know that."

"Well, yeah I do." He felt sorry for his cousin. The kid was so alone. It was true, he didn't know what he would do if both his folks died suddenly. "Cale, you are facing a lot right now. You're seventeen with a family that hardly knows you and you don't know them."

Cale coughed but said nothing.

"I know you care for my folks and they care for you. But shit man, you basically popped into our lives a year and a half ago and this town is in the middle of nowhere."

Cale took a deep breath but continued his silence.

"You play rugby, which is cool, but you don't play hockey."

"They didn't have hockey in Texas."

"Well they do in Hanna. Just like a million other things that are different. At least you like hunting." Jace gave a hug. "Hey, I know you didn't have a choice on any of this. I know you feel like you're all alone."

"I have friends. Plus you, Uncle Joe and Aunt Katy."

"You do have me cuz, but I live in Toronto. It's how it is. Mom and Dad want the best for you, but they're still getting to know you. That is loud and clear even without this locket scene. It is just a symptom."

"What should I do Jace? I mean I really am sorry I said those awful things to Aunt Katy."

"Apology will go a long ways and the two of you will have a better understanding. But my mother and my father, as much as I love them want nothing more than to live and die in Hanna. They give no encouragement about the future even though you can have a great life."

"I don't understand."

"Cale, first of all, in case no one has told you, at twenty one, you are going to inherit a shit load of money. Your folks weren't poor. Second, my mother is great, but she didn't want to go to university, nor my dad. They are glad you are doing well in school, but I bet there has been no mention about college or university."

"No, but I'm not sure what I'm doing."

"Well, get your ass out of here. Dude, I know enough about your inheritance to tell you, eighteen, a year from now, you can go to any college you want in the world and it will be covered. The further away from here the better."

"Really? I could go anywhere?"

"All you have to do is get the grades and get accepted."

"Jace, I didn't know any of this."

"Probably not." Jace put the locket in Cale's hand.

"I should give it back to Aunt Katy."

"Nah, she's cool. If I were you, I'd give it to that special lady that is going to come into your life. Until then, use it as a reminder of our talk out here on the plains outside Hanna. Remember, this day as the time I told you to leave this place when you can and go find out what Cale O'Rourke is meant to do in this world."

"Jace, I don't know what to say. You have helped me so much today."

"Well, I guess I just did something pretty radical myself."

"What do you mean?"

"I've joined the military. I get to use my shooting skills for more than just deer."

"Wow."

"Yeah, Mom and Dad aren't thrilled because I could be anywhere but here. But I hate to say, that is half the appeal."

"But I won't be able to visit you."

"Well we have to see what happens. But you don't need to be near me. Hell, I'd move to Australia if I were you."

A year and half later, Cale was attending Queensland University in Brisbane.

CHAPTER 10

Taipei, Taiwan
The Distant Past

Vesper was excited. Jay had called and was coming over to tell her something of great consequence. She hoped it was a marriage proposal.

Jay Chou was almost ten years older, but she found him young in attitude and looks. She laughed with him all the time. Jay was a fantastic lover, and at the age, when men's families expected them to marry. He was almost too good to be true. She had given him her heart along with her virginity.

Vesper knew his family might resist having her as a daughter-in-law because she was not pure Chinese, but once they realized how much Jay and she loved each other, it would work out. She'd give him beautiful children, be a good mother and an excellent, supportive wife.

Three years ago, Vesper had been attending Dong-hai University and modeling part time. She had walked into Sogo Department store on the day she met Jay to buy a tie for her father's birthday. While shopping, she had noticed Jay in an expensive department, buying a pair of posh dress shoes. She made a note of his handsomeness and continued to her destination. He turned up at the tie shop and mistook her for a salesgirl. Vesper accepted his dinner invitation to apologize for his mistake.

Her thoughts were interrupted by a knock at the door. She shared the apartment with two other girls, but both were gone to their family's homes for the weekend. She had the place to herself.

She looked through the security hole. It was Jay. He had a small box wrapped in brown paper under his arm.

"Shey de dongxi?" (Who is that for?)

"Ni." (You.) She opened the door. They embraced, kissed and then he handed her the brown wrapped box with both hands. She was now beside herself with joy. Vesper tore the paper off and found a black velvet box. Inside there was a heart-shaped locket. It was beautiful, but it was not a ring.

"She wan ma?" (Like it?) Jay looked into her face ready to receive a kiss.

"She wan. Hen paliong." (I like. Very beautiful.) She couldn't contain her disappointment.

"Zeme le?" (Anything wrong?) Jay asked quietly. He closed the door.

Vesper shook her head. She was being silly. The locket gleamed in her hand.

"Hey. Sheme?" (What?)

"Wo jeuda hen bun. Wo sysang niger syungzr yo jyair." (I feel stupid. I thought the box had a ring.)

"Huh? Weisema?" (Why?) Jay was surprised. "Ni jr dow bu keyi jia hoon ni, dwei bu dwei?" (You know I can't marry you right?)

She looked up. She couldn't believe what she was hearing.

"Weisema?" (Why?) She barely got the word out.

"Inwei, ni de baba shr Meigwo ren. Wo de mama hen baba bu yao Weigoren syai yai." (Because your father is American. My mother and father don't want foreign blood.) Jay was surprised she didn't realize that. Wives in Taiwan were very important to the family. He had to choose a woman that would be beyond reproach. He did love Vesper, but her blood was not pure. That was just how it was. He would never bring her into his family.

Vesper was shocked and angry. This was crazy. How could the man she loved say these hurtful words to her?

"Ni jr dow wo ai ni. Gou le. Wo jeuda women lyung timg pay he." (You know I love you. It is enough. I feel we are good together.) Jay spoke softly. He wanted to get into the bedroom. Vesper was wonderful in bed.

She turned away.

Jay put his hand on her shoulder. "Kwai dian chin wo." (Quickly kiss me.)

"Bu yao." (I don't want.) Vesper felt her insides go numb. This man was using her. She felt confused and realized he was trying to make her feel stupid. Jay would not get away with this.

"Kwai dian, chin wo." (Quickly kiss me.) Jay said again louder. He didn't like this disrespect.

Vesper turned to him hiding her anger. She smiled when she saw he could not detect it. He only had one thing on his mind.

"Sorry," she said in English. Vesper gave Jay a soft, tender kiss on the lips. As she kissed him, Vesper realized he must die. It was a surprisingly easy decision.

"Bang mang wo." (Help me.) Vesper said as she held

up the locket.

Jay put it around her neck and kissed her.

Vesper gave a small, involuntary shudder. Quietly she said, "Zenme shung-chuan hao ma?" (How about we go to bed?)

"Hao, wo syung gern-nee zai zechee." (Good, I want to make love to you.) Jay said.

Vesper turned and smiled at Jay. "Danisha. Wo yao wo dianhua de punyo." (Wait. I want to call my friend.)

Jay believed the trouble had passed, that he was in control again.

"Shenzai ma?" (Now?) Jay wanted to go to bed now. He had to leave in an hour. This needed to be a quick encounter.

"Ichian, wo gausu ta, wo dianhua. Wo bu yao ta dianhua zai shr-wu fun zhong." (Before, I told her I would call. I don't want her to call in fifteen minutes.)

Jay nodded, kissed her lightly on the lips and followed her to the small bedroom.

Vesper went to the phone and dialed the number she seldom called. When it was answered she spoke in English.

"Uncle John, this is Vesper."

"Vesper?! Weisema ni show Engwen?" (Vesper! Why are you speaking English?)

"Because I must. There is someone here... I don't want them to understand my words." Vesper hoped her uncle was going to be receptive. She had never asked for anything like this before, but then again, she had never felt like this.

"O.K.," the voice on the end of the line said, gravely.

"I have made a mistake and been dishonored by a

man. He is treating me like a toy. He tells me because of my blood I am not worthy to be his wife, yet he waits for me in the bedroom as we speak." She knew he could understand, her uncle's English was better than hers.

Hu An Shan (John Hu) was a very well connected man. He had several businesses in Taiwan and Hong Kong that were supported by one of the largest criminal organizations in Asia. In China, "guanshi" (who you know) was key to success in business. It always helped to know someone in the government or on the police force, but it was essential to have a connection with the underworld as well.

"So you are calling me for what?" Her uncle's voice was crackly from static on the other end.

"I want him gone." Vesper's voice had gotten quieter. She was decisive with her plan.

"There are many ways to be gone." The line became clearer.

"I know. He needs to understand that his intentions with me were dishonorable and he insulted my family." Vesper knew her uncle was a strong family man.

"I can't do this to every man that breaks your heart."

"I will do it myself now if you won't." Vesper's voice said lowly.

"Don't even say those stupid words. Kick him out and we'll talk about this next week, the phone is not a good idea."

It was happening.

"First, I will go into the bedroom and sleep with him so that he thinks everything is O.K."

"You can do that?" The line threw out a small blast of static.

"I am a Hu. I have my mother's family name, not my father's." It was the only way the Hu family would accept a mixed marriage.

John Hu felt pride. He had no children. Vesper was the only mixed blood child in the family and she had turned into a beautiful woman.

"Vesper, I will take care of it. However, I would like one favor."

Vesper felt her throat get tight. Jay was going to die. "Yes?"

"Let's have dinner and talk about business. You are about to graduate."

"Business?"

"I have an investment opportunity. But only a strong, beautiful and smart woman can make it successful."

"I'm not sure what you are saying."

"Have dinner with me in the next week. Your aunt will be happy to see you."

Vesper knew her prior life was over. She put her hand on the new locket. It would not be a token of Jay's feeling for her, but a symbol of the day she changed her life knowingly.

"Uncle it will be a pleasure to come and visit."

"We'll talk later."

Vesper put down the phone and went to the bedroom. Jay was stretched out on the bed naked.

Vesper unbuttoned her blouse as she walked over to the bed.

Jay rubbed his stomach with his left hand and said loudly, "Kwai dian." (Quickly.)

She smiled at him. The blouse came off. He should

be taking his time. Vesper leaned down and kissed his ear and touched his stomach next to his hand with gentleness. "Danisha." (Wait a moment.) She whispered in his ear.

"Ni sirle wo." (You're killing me.) As he felt her hand go lower down his stomach.

Quietly Vesper said, "Jr dow."(I know.)

Twenty years, and three broken chains later, the locket now had condensed beads of sweat on it. It dangled between her damp, bare breasts. To this day she put it on to steel herself for tough business situations. She needed to own this man who was now staring at her locket. Why was he staring at the locket? For some reason it made her uncomfortable.

(One Month Later)

Nick handed the taxi driver 300 NT.

The longhaired young man looked at the money. The meter read 180. He wasn't sure what to do.

Nick saw the question and said, "Shou Fei." (Tip.) He knew this word well.

The young man smiled. "Shei shei." He said thanking the Westerner.

Cale stepped out into the warm, muggy tropical air behind Nick.

"I don't think you get it, Cale,"

"I get a lot…" Cale was angry, "but not this shit."

"You want to come up to my place and talk about it?" They were in front of Nick's apartment building. Cale's hotel was only a short walk away.

"Don't know if I should." Cale looked down at the

ground.

"Fuck you, asshole."

"That's exactly what I'm trying to prevent." Cale said quietly, still looking down.

Nick shook his head and said loudly, "Don't wrap me up in a nice little package, Cale."

"I couldn't wrap you up in any package. You don't tell me all that much. I'm just going by what I see." Cale looked up into Nick's face. The red light on the corner turned green.

Nick took a deep breath. "Cale, I like you. Really. But I'm not going to open myself up to how I tick on all counts, after two months." Nick's voice was cold. Cale O'Rourke was saying all the wrong things right now.

A small yellow Ford taxi beeped at them and slowed down, speeding-up after no acknowledgement from the men.

"Nick you just tried to have some sort of sex with me. How do you think I'm supposed to feel?" Cale watched Nick's face.

"I'll say it one last time, and you better listen, Cowboy Cale. You are being paid to do whatever these ladies want."

"Bullshit!" Cale yelled. "If they told me to stab you I wouldn't do that either."

Nick tilted his head and smiled. "Really, you wouldn't stick me with a knife? Guess this is why I like you Cale."

"Nick," Cale said trying to keep his anger in check. "You act like you know everything about everyone, yet no one is supposed to understand you, because you're way too cool."

"So I'm *cool* now."

"Yeah, you were until you…" Cale didn't want to say anymore. He was exasperated.

"Until I grabbed your dick, like I was told to, by the paying ladies." Nick put on a mocking smile,

"Look…"

"No, Cale, you look. This work you're in right now means you deliver sex and fantasy. Knives aren't involved. Sex is!" Nick coughed a little as he went on. "This isn't some lark you get to have as you try and learn about yourself. These women expect to get what they pay for and if you can't deliver, quit now, because some of these ladies are crazy. Crazy!"

"I won't do gay stuff."

"Then quit because you don't understand the world you are in. " Nick shook his head. "What did you think was going to happen when they bought us together? Don't forget, I tried to stop it."

Cale remembered back. It was true. He hadn't seen any harm when the three ladies had bought them out, together. Nick had objected but was over ruled by Vesper.

"You knew their intentions and didn't say anything?!" The question was an accusation.

"Hey, what makes me know you so well, I knew you didn't want it to happen?"

"Huh? What?"

"You must have known we'd be in bed together or something like that. There were three of them and two of us. Do the math. Something weird was going to go down."

Cale looked at Nick. "But you didn't even hesitate

when they told you to grab my dick."

"Nope, I didn't." Nick stared at Cale in the eyes, his voice deadpan.

"How far were you going to go with me?" Cale choked out the words. He was still angry, but not just with Nick. Cale knew this was a fucked up world but tonight had been just plain weird.

"Guess it depended on what the ladies wanted."

"You'd really let a dollar amount control you like that?"

Nick sighed. This was almost a stupid conversation. "Are you standing in judgment of me, Cale? You have a sanitized idea of what a ladies man is, I guess." Nick reached in and pulled his keys out of his pants pocket.

Cale flushed in the dark. It was true. This wasn't American Gigolo.

"You still have that bottle of Sauza I saw last week?" Cale asked as he watched Nick make eye contact.

"I do." Nick kept his eyes on Cale.

"I could use a shot right now."

Nick slightly nodded and said quietly "Yeah, me too."

Together they walked into the apartment entrance in silence. They stayed silent until Nick opened his front door. He turned on the light.

Cale went to the comfortable chair in the corner.

Nick brought a bottle of Sauza, two shot glasses and a bottle of French mineral water. He poured two shots.

"Cheers," he said raising his glass to Cale, seated across from him.

Both downed the mild liquid fire and shook their

heads. Nick opened the bottle of water and offered it to Cale first. Cale took it and chugged a couple gulps and handed it back to Nick.

"Well…" Cale's voice trailed off. He didn't know what to say.

"Let's smoke a joint." Nick got up.

"I don't smoke, you know that." Cale said watching him.

"Might be a good night to start." Nick sat back down with a rolled cigarette.

"Thanks, I'll pass."

Nick lit the cigarette. "Suit yourself." He then took a deep drag.

"How many times have you done this?"

"Getting high alone?"

"No, don't play with me, Nick. Done this stuff with men?"

"Stuff with men?" Nick took another drag. His mood was lightening.

"Yeah, you know."

"Cale stop being a loser right now." Nick said exhaling. "Stand by your guns and think the worst, but fucking spit out what you want to know."

"I don't know what I want to know. I really don't. But how can you be so fucking nonchalant about all this shit? " Cale brushed his hair back.

"There was a time Cale, my career as a dancer sometimes depended upon my skills as a hustler. I got money and jobs because I'd let people put coke on my dick and lick it off." Nick took another drag.

"Men?" Cale could barely say the word.

"Men fall under the category of people." Nick looked to the ground.

"I'll take a hit off that." Cale reached out.

Nick smiled and handed it to Cale. His first hit made him cough.

"Virgin." Nick laughed.

Cale grinned and took another hit, but much smaller.

"Hold it in." Nick continued to smile.

Cale handed it back feeling a little tingle.

"It never seemed wrong to you?"

"It seemed wrong to let something like society's judgments keep me from getting what I wanted."

"I don't get it."

"Cale, you aren't a dancer. I am straight or I'd tell you different. I don't have time to be something I'm not, unless you're paying with a job or money." Nick took a drag and handed it to Cale.

Another inhale, a bit bigger. Cale felt a cough coming on and he let it out in a compressed nasal blast.

"You sound so jaded, bro." Cale handed back the almost finished joint.

Nick finished it in two tokes. "This is coming from a guy who is doing what?"

Cale sighed. "You're right. But you were pretty young…"

"Don't over think it Cale. The first couple times were hard, but I either needed a job or money pretty badly." Nick poured two more shots.

"I can see why you don't talk about your life." Cale felt himself becoming a little light-headed. It felt good.

Nick handed a shot to his friend. "What we are talking about is just scratching the surface of my life."

Cale said quietly. "It is hard to talk to most people. I am glad you talk to me."

"Losing your folks and ya, the bomb story is pretty tough." Nick picked up his glass. "Cheers, again."

"You've been a hustler since you were seventeen?"

"Some people might say that."

"How else can you say it?"

"I'd call me an opportunist." Nick sighed. "My home life was less than desirable with my two brothers in jail along with my folks. I didn't have a family exactly. A lot of foster homes." Nick scratched his head. "But I did discover pretty early I could dance. So dancer I became. Short version, I left school as soon as I could. Went to Vegas to get work and experience."

"At seventeen?"

"Cale, I'll admit I was a kid, but a kid who already knew a lot about the world." Nick lowered his voice and added. "At least I thought I did."

"What's that mean?"

"Jesus, Cale. Do you want to see the mole on my balls too?"

"If I'd hung out a little longer tonight with you and the ladies, I guess I'd have seen it soon enough." Cale smiled at his own joke.

"O.K., smart guy." Nick laughed at Cale. Then his tone got serious. "I was drugged my first time where I got paid. I didn't know it was going to happen." Nick shut his eyes.

"Do you want to keep talking about this?"

"Not really," Nick said, his eyes shut. "Cale, I used

my body for bartering purposes. From that same bullshit encounter I just told you about. I got my first paying dancing job. A couple hundred bucks was huge for me fresh out of high school. I guess it started a cycle."

"So that's how you started." Cale was hesitant with his question.

"If you mean *started* in the sex trade or dancing professionally, the answer to both is yes. A month later, thank God, I found out women paid quite well and appreciated my dancing too. I got jobs because of gigs and vice-versa."

"How old are you?"

"Ten years past my first pay-off."

"Haven't you been affected by all this?"

"Of course, Cale!" Nick looked at the man across from him. "I'm probably really fucked up. But I have no illusions about what I'm doing. It's all about the reward in the end."

"Are the ladies really going to expect us two to have sex?" Cale said shaking his head.

"We'll try to keep it to a minimum." Nick winked at him.

"It really doesn't bother you?"

"Not at all. What bothers me is I haven't got to fuck Apple. She's bought me out twice this month and sent me home after a couple of drinks. I'd totally do that woman for free."

"She is fucking hot. Wish she'd buy me out."

"Maybe she'll buy us out together. What are you going to do then, bro?" Nick laughed.

Cale nodded and said, "Whatever she wants. Whatever she wants." They laughed together.

Sitting back into his chair, Cale looked over at Nick who was smiling. "Can we smoke another joint?"

Nick got up to get his stash in the kitchen and said over his shoulder, "Let's go out to some club and dance."

"I don't dance."

Nick walked back, "That, my boy, is about to change. Babes love a guy who can dance, strip and fuck."

"I don't strip either."

"Cale, this night is getting a little old on all things you don't do. Can't you just take my cue and see what happens?"

Cale sighed. "Can we just smoke a fucking joint? That's already one massive rule I've broken tonight."

Nick quickly rolled a hash joint, took a drag and handed it to Cale. "I'm going to get you really stoney and we're going dancing." He let out a chuckle.

Cale nodded, smiled and let the warm, fuzzy feeling take over.

CHAPTER 11

Taichung, Taiwan
One Month Later

"So just tell the taxi *gong gong che* and then say Free-Go, that's the company name. And it's 8:30 A.M., like I said before." On the phone to Cale, Brian sounded like a camp counselor, or maybe a math teacher.

Cale used his shoulder to keep his phone pressed against his ear. He was going through his clothes, sorting a load of laundry that had just been returned to his hotel room. "And he'll just drop me off at the right bus stop?" He was going to ignore the jibe at possible tardiness.

"Don't get out of the cab until you see me at the side of the road, standing next to a lot of really big green buses."

Cale gave a little cough, "So what do you look like?"

There was a pause on the other end of the line, "I'll be the guy next to the green buses, probably the only tall one who is not Chinese. See you tomorrow. Don't be late." There was a click as the line went dead. He had hung-up on Cale.

"What an asshole." Cale said under his breath. He looked at his phone as he closed it in his hand. The name Brian was written in LCD on its tiny screen. "Nick was right." He remembered Nick warning him about Brian.

Cale had extended his visa at the local police station, but he couldn't do that again. Nick had mentioned something called a 'visa run' before. It involved going to Taipei, but beyond that, it was a mystery.

Cale's questions on the matter had evoked a sarcastic response from Nick, "Brian will explain it to you."

Nick looked bored as Vesper pushed a large manila envelope across the table to Cale.

"Be nice, Nick. Not everyone is such a kind guy as you." Vesper said with her own touch of sarcasm. Turning to Cale, "Take this and your passport, Brian will explain everything. He has helped me with Nick a few times. You must go tomorrow." Vesper now smiled as she stood up. "I'll be right back."

"So this guy Brian will explain it all for me?" Cale asked as he watched Vesper go out the door

"Ya, Brian will explain everything – everything in the fucking universe and then some - if you're stupid enough to listen to the guy." Nick spat.

"Is he bad?" Cale was surprised.

"Loser with a capital L! To hear the guy talk is like hearing an encyclopedia. He's a smart guy but he's a fucking flake." Nick took out a cigarette from his pack as he continued, "I will say he had a wicked hot girlfriend. I think I heard they broke up not too long ago." Nick lit his cigarette.

"What do you mean by 'flake'?" Cale looked at him.

"I think she goes to the university where he teaches." Nick's mind was still on Brian's ex.

Vesper came back to the teashop booth. She leaned over the table slightly to pull in her chair. Her necklace dangled over her exposed cleavage.

131

"What's the night-life like in Taipei?"

Vesper sighed, "Please, Cale. You will be able to do this fast. Don't try to spend too much time in Taipei. It's such a dirty city."

Nick stretched his neck and turned to Cale "Three hours on the bus, three hours Taipei, and three hours back. If it doesn't rain the whole time you're there it's probably the one day out of the year the weather isn't shit."

"You guys make the place seem very inviting." Cale had heard the weather in Taipei was much worse than Tai-chung.

"See for yourself. Get Brian to take you out." Nick was sarcastic.

"Maybe I will." Cale decided he was going to make his own decision about Taipei.

The next day he was up and at the bus station a few minutes early. As early as he was, Cale saw a tall man standing beside a green bus. After paying the driver, he walked over to his contact.

It was almost a surreal image, the tall foreigner standing in khakis and a grey golf shirt next to a fleet of green buses with "FREE-GO" written across them. Brian smiled as he approached.

"I'm Brian." He extended his open hand, high as though they were on a basketball court. He held a briefcase.

"Cale O'Rourke."

"Vesper said you were new. Your first visa run?" Brian slung his black backpack over his shoulder and motioned for them to walk towards the bus.

"Here's your ticket. The bus is ready to go."

Together they got on the large bus. Cale could see

by the wear and tear of the gray cloth seats, the vehicle had seen better days.

Brian sat next to him.

"How does all this shit work?" Cale was growing uneasy with his own ignorance as the bus left the station to Taipei. The bus smelled vaguely of piss and he was growing hungry. He had skipped breakfast.

Cale looked out the window as Brian unpacked a Subway Sub.

"You have to start thinking of yourself as an alien. We are going to Federal police headquarters to make sure the Taiwanese government knows where you are."

"This is just an extension, right?"

"More or less." Brian broke his sandwich in half. "You want some?"

Cale took it gratefully. "Thanks."

Maybe this guy wasn't so bad.

He finished swallowing the first bite and asked. "So what is this school Flagler?"

"They are a real school. They just take students that don't always come to class." Brian laughed quietly. Then he said, "Flagler will give you a certificate saying you are studying Chinese. This will allow the police to extend your visa." Brian took a bite of his sandwich.

"Don't the police care it's fake?" Cale took another bite. Nick might not like Brian, but other than his phone manner, he seemed like a decent guy.

"There is usually some payoff by the school to the police." Brian seemed surprised how naïve this guy was. "You know that happens over here."

"Yeah, I guess. I don't really know. Haven't ever lived

in a place where it was like this."

"Don't you work for Vesper?"

"So?"

"Cale, are you really this much a babe in the woods?" Brian's voice was condescending.

"Hey man, screw you."

"I don't know why you're getting upset; I don't look down on it or anything…" Brian looked straight ahead as he talked. His face was emotionless.

"Thanks for that. It makes me feel a lot better knowing you don't look down on me." Cale finished his half too and likewise threw away his trash in the netting in front of him. There was silence between them for almost an hour.

"Cale you are going to have to talk to me sometime soon. You are worse than Nick and I didn't think that was possible." Brian looked over at his charge.

"Yeah, well I don't think Nick has any love for you either." Cale was starting to dislike Brian immensely.

"Breaks my heart to hear that." Brian's voice was hard. "He thinks he is God's gift to the world because he has a lot of sex."

"When's the last time you got laid? You sound like you need to." Cale's face matched Brian's lack of emotion.

"I don't get laid – I do the laying, my friend." Brian motioned to the Taipei Train Station looming in front. The city's grey sky greeted them. "Look, I don't need this attitude as I'm doing you a favor."

"Aren't you getting paid for this?"

"Not enough." The bus pulled into the station.

Both disembarked in silence.

"It's not that far. We can walk from here." Brian's voice was terse. They walked for about ten minutes in silence.

"Is it much further?" Cale stopped in the middle of his stride. He was still hungry, tired and questioning why he was in Taiwan again.

"No, it's not. We'll get you fixed up fine so you don't have to leave your job banging cougars." Brian didn't like this guy at all. He seemed like a crybaby.

"You think I care about the job? I don't give a shit. I can leave this country today if they say I can't get the visa." Cale's brow came low over his eyes. "I don't give a shit about anything right now."

Brian stopped and turned to face him. They were on a crossing bridge over a major street. Hundreds of cars and scooters moved beneath them and pedestrians moved around them as if they were medians.

"I don't really give a shit either Cale. I'm out of this country in a couple months. But if you want to make Vesper happy, you'll come to Flagler and get your attendance filled out and then go the police station. We'll get your stamp and then they won't come and arrest you and we don't ever have to see each other again."

"Look, man, I don't want to fight with you or anything. I realize you're going out of your way here, I – I just had a rough night and morning and…" Cale felt nauseous from the city fumes below.

Brian was surprised at the apology.

"Cale, let's start over. I've been a bit of an asshole, too." Brian continued, "After we get you fixed up, let's grab lunch. I know a great place."

Cale nodded and smiled. They started to walk towards Flagler school.

CHAPTER 12

Three Weeks Later

"Nick you always make me laugh." Barbara Profit picked up her joint and lit it.

"Just got that type of face, huh?" Nick chuckled at her.

She handed him the recently rolled hash cigarette. Barbara held in the smoke and felt her mood lighten. She liked being in Nick's company.

Nick took a deep drag. He held the smoke in his lungs.

He was so damn good looking.

Exhaling, Nick looked at her and said, "Great stuff, Barb."

She smiled at him and took the joint. "You free for some beers?" Barbara asked hoping he would say he could.

"I don't know. I'm definitely gonna take the night off and maybe do something with Cale." He scratched his nose. The smoke was irritating it.

"You two spend almost every day together."

"Most of the time it's work. Our nights out are actually rare." He took the joint back. Nick was high. "You can join us." Nick said as he took another drag, the joint was half finished.

"Don't you think I'd be in the way?" Barbara smiled at Nick. She really wanted to kiss him.

"In the way? We're just going to hang out and drink – no big thing." He handed her the joint after hitting it one more time.

Barbara pulled the joint from her mouth and asked quietly with hesitation, "Nick, do you think we'll ever..." She couldn't finish her sentence. She wanted to blame it on being stoned but she knew better.

Nick Young looked at her and smiled. Barb was no stunner, but pretty enough, although a little heavy for his taste. They had been together once, well over a year ago. He had almost put it out of his mind, for no real reason, it was just too many women ago and nothing spectacular.

"Barb what's up here?" he smiled with confidence. "You want a little action?" Nick let out a small snigger. Barb gave him the nub of the smoking joint. He would get the last hit.

"Hey, it's not easy for a Western lady to hook-up here. You know how it is." She stared in his chocolate brown eyes.

"You mean us guys always with the Asian beauty leaving you poor Western ladies with nothing." He killed the joint in an ashtray and let out the smoke. Nick felt great. Barbara was a good lady, plus he liked she didn't charge him full price when he got drugs from her. "That story is so old." Nick laughed.

"Make light of it, go without sex for months at a time and see how your mood stays." She looked up at the ceiling of her studio apartment.

Nick stood up and undid his pants. They fell to his

knees. Next he pulled down his boxers.

"Jesus, what are you doing?!" Barb laughed as she saw his naked lower body.

He smiled again and reached down and grabbed himself. "Next hour, this is yours."

"You're all about the hour aren't you?" Barb said looking into his face. Why did she have to be so drawn to him? She looked back down at his hand.

"And you're all for Profit. Aren't you, Barbara?" Nick moved a little closer starting to stroke now.

Barb looked from his hand to his knockout face.

"Guess I have to take a mercy fuck when I can." She wished he'd tell her she wasn't a mercy fuck but no words came, only his breathing.

"Fuck you." Barb said under her breath as she reached for what his hand was holding.

"You will and you're gonna like it."

Nick stepped out onto the sidewalk, filled with parked scooters, just outside of Barbara's apartment lobby. After a cab ride home, he showered and was dressing when his phone rang. It was Vesper.

"Nick, nee how." Vesper's voice sounded playful, inflected. She'd been hanging around Taichung a lot since Cale had come to town.

"Wode hen hao pengyo lai Taichung. Tamen yao ..." (My good friends have come to Taichung. They want...) - Vesper's voice was cut-off by a cacophonous blast of female laughter. Vesper switched to English. "They seem a little," there was more laughter, distorting the phone. "They seem so lonely!" Vesper laughed herself into the phone; she sounded a bit drunk. He had only seen her drunk three times – all within the last two months.

"Meet you at Escapade?" Nick checked his watch; it said 7:15 PM.

"No, my apartment. You know where it is. Please bring Cale." Vesper whispered into the phone.

"I'm at the pool." Cale said, towel drying his hair with one hand and holding the cell phone to his ear with his shoulder. He and Nick had recently become flat mates and he guessed Nick needed something from the store.

"I just got a phone call from Vesper. She wants us for some VIPs." Nick finished dressing with the exception of finding a sweater. "At her apartment."

"I thought Vesper lived in Taipei?" Cale said as he collected his things from the lounge chair. "She seems like she is here all the time."

"Ya, she's been around a lot lately. As in, a lot since you've been in town." Nick sounded distracted as he pulled out a blue cotton sweater from his dresser.

"So you're saying she's addicted to my skills?"

"Ya, your dick has real talent." Nick didn't see any reason to tell Cale, Vesper might be around because she was watching him to see if he played cowboy again.

"Well, once you lay them right the first time, you can walk on them forever. I guess I'm a natural." The exaggerated cockiness came through loud and clear over the cell phone.

"Is this the same guy who was scared to fuck his first spa girl a couple months ago?" Nick was cut-off by Cale's laughter.

"You! It's all your fault I'm this fucking sex magnet now."

"What number is this going to be? 58 or 59?"

"66 Mr. Young."

"So Mr. Fucking Sex Magnet, looks like we got VIP action tonight with Vesper in tow. Get your party hat on."

The drinking game wasn't going well for Cale.

"You lose again. Gambei!" Vesper shouted gleefully. She was enjoying getting Cale drunk. Vesper had not ever seen him not in control and he was actually cute. This could be useful later to her plans for this evening. Violet and Jie were a bit drunk too, but they were not even close to Cale's level of intoxication.

"Vesper why don't we do something else besides play drinking games?" Nick asked as he watched his friend throw down another shot of Cordon Bleu Cognac. "What a waste of good liquor." Nick thought to himself. It was high grade spirits meant to be sipped out of a brandy snifter.

"We are having a good time. But maybe we should play gambei for clothes. A stripping game." Vesper got a mischievous smile. Cale would soon be naked and drunk. The perfect plaything. He might not even get a hard-on, but that could be fun too. Cale would have to satisfy in other ways. That is why she had arranged this little party for Jie Chen. Cale O Rourke would learn she was not a businessperson to mess with.

Nick was aware what Vesper was doing once he saw Jie was involved. She was a crazy bitch who liked to cause physical pain. Her nails were legend amongst the other men who worked for Vesper.

He once himself had been raked so badly by Jie, it took over a week before he could look in the mirror and not see her marks. Nick shrugged his shoulders and walked over to the stereo. He looked at what CD's he could dance to. Nick saw a remix of an early Fatboy Slim. He looked over the titles and then over to the group drinking.

"Not again!" Cale moaned as he felt the high from the cognac kicking in stronger.

"O.K., take off your shirt." Jie Chen squealed with delight. She was a pretty woman of thirty-four who owned a decorating company in Kaushong. Jie was only in town for the day and she was eyeing this man as her companion later. Vesper had insinuated this new one would be hers for the night.

Cale rubbed his head. Then in one motion pulled off his sports shirt and sat down bare-chested, tossing his shirt on the floor.

Apple Lu smiled. This new guy, Cale, had a good body. She liked his face too. Looking down at her nicely manicured nails, Apple had to admit she was very attracted. It had been a long time.

Vesper looked over at Nick who had just put the Fatboy Slim CD on.

"What are you doing?" Vesper demanded as she looked back at Cale. She knew Jie was going to buy him out. Vesper toyed with the idea of being with Cale herself, as she saw him sitting there being so boyishly cute. However, that didn't suit her plans. It depended on how the evening went. She was a bit drunk and it was time to slow down. Since Cale had joined the game, slowing down had been easier.

The music started.

Jie was watching Cale. She knew better than to pursue Nick.

He had made it clear to Vesper he would never be with Jie again.

Jie knew she was crazy when it came to sex. Inflicting pain was how she got off. It was twisted but satisfying. She smiled as she looked at Cale's wide chest.

"Vesper is a cold bitch for setting this whole scene up." Thought Nick.

Nick smiled as he looked at Apple. She was looking hot tonight in her tight black dress. He hoped she would take him tonight, but doubted it. Violet, who was rich, always bought him if he was up for grabs. It was a given. The few times Apple had bought him out, they had never even kissed, much less had sex. From what he knew, she never had sex with any of the guys she bought. She was well known for being that way. It seemed she just liked to party and didn't mind paying for the company. Nick waited a few seconds for the beat to kick in.

"Nick what are you doing?" Vesper asked again.

Cale lost once more.

Vesper's attention went back to Cale.

"This really was going to be too easy." Vesper thought to herself. Jie had herself a victim who wasn't going to be able to put up much of a fight. This would teach him and Nick their independence of recent times didn't please her.

"I might dance a little while you folks drink." He looked her straight in Vesper's eyes.

Cale was kicking off his shoes as he said quietly, "I'm

definitely not getting lucky tonight." Cale drank his shot.

"Maybe you will be later," Jie's laughed giving Nick the creeps.

Vesper smiled. Jie was someone she liked as a person. She knew Cale was probably going to come to her tomorrow and complain about what Jie did in bed with him. At least she hoped so. It had always happened before. The last man Jie had bought from Escapade, had to see a doctor the day after.

Cale gazed at Jie and smiled with a juvenile look.

Vesper chuckled, "Cale I think you are getting drunk."

Cale's smile brightened.

"Hey Apple, come dance with me," Nick said motioning for her to join him.

Apple wasn't sure about moving. She was enjoying being around the new guy Cale, even though she had the impression Jie was buying him tonight.

"Come on," Nick moved his hips in a slow inviting manner.

Apple was charmed, but she wasn't buying Nick tonight because she had to be up early in the morning. Besides, Violet was here and the woman had a thing for Nick. He'd be double the price if he was available. She got up and walked to where Nick was dancing to the music. Apple had to admit he had moves.

Nick pulled her to him closely. He said quietly, "You have to buy Cale tonight. Jie is nothing but big trouble."

"You are the one that brought him." Apple kept her voice low.

"I would never have, if I'd known Jie was at this party. Vesper knows that too. I think she is playing some sort of bad game with me and my friend."

"Nick, I don't understand. I only came over to dance." Apple's protest was not for real. She was intrigued.

Nick sighed as he pulled her closer to his body. He kept his voice low. "Apple, we've hung out a few times and I know you are a good person." Nick went into a whisper above the music. "Trust me on this. Cale is a good guy and Vesper is totally wrong to allow him to be bought by Jie."

They both turned and looked over at Cale. He was getting out of his pants. There was a big smile on his face.

Nick continued, "Seriously, I don't want Cale to have what happened to me when Jie took me to bed. It's ugly, painful and she's almost dangerous. I'll pay whatever it costs. Just don't let Jie get him tonight. I'll talk to Cale and Vesper about this tomorrow, but now is not the right time."

"He's from Canada, isn't he?" Apple looked at the man who was sitting in his underwear laughing. She was definitely attracted to this stranger.

"Find out for yourself. I'm serious; I'll pay. Just do it now before this gets out of hand." Nick took in a whiff of Apple's smell. "Very nice," he thought to himself.

"O.K. I'll get him out of here." Apple Lu had lived most of her twenty-seven years around North York, Canada. Although Western in upbringing and attitude, she still felt a strong tie to her Chinese ancestry. The combination made her more sensitive to how people ticked. Nick was puzzling her. She enjoyed his company when they went out, but this nobility was making her like him very much.

"Thank you," Nick said relieved.

"He's lucky to have you as a friend."

145

"I don't know. He wouldn't be here if I hadn't brought him." Nick took in another breath of her scent.

"That's not really your fault. I heard Vesper ask for Cale." Apple kept her eyes on Cale as he was motioned for a pause to the game.

"Ya and I'm not standing on the sidelines as I watch this go down."

"You aren't. You've taken care of the situation." Apple's voice went to a whisper, "Just watch out about showing this caring side. It makes you very sexy and you are too sexy already."

"Maybe you should buy us both." Nick kidded. He knew his night was going to be with Violet.

"Sorry. The time May, Candy and Alice bought you both is famous. Cale freaked out. Any woman who buys you two together has to have a show that is not PG-13. Not sure I'm up for that tonight."

"You could just pretend we did a show."

"Yeah, I could, but I would want to see a performance." Apple laughed a little. "I'll get Cale out of here if you pay but I don't think you can afford to pay for both of you, right?"

"You're right." Nick smiled. "There would be a lot of attention on our little evening together if we both left with you. We asked not to be turned into pseudo gay love dolls."

"Vesper agreed?"

"She didn't really. I guess it has to happen eventually."

"I kiss women all the time in my job. We are expected to touch each other and there is plenty of same sex with

146

women." Apple's voice purred, "Men love it. Why can't we women purchase the same thing?"

"I know. If you are paying, you are entitled. But there are limits. Jie is one those people who goes too far." Nick's voice went low, "Cale has his limits and they should be respected. He is pretty willing to do everything else."

"This is why Vesper is setting him up with Jie." Apple could see that.

"Ya well, it's a stupid move if she wants him to stay."

"Maybe she doesn't him to stay. He's tested her authority and given you a reason to be a wild card." Apple had heard that Nick had been a problem for Vesper since Cale had arrived.

"O.K., makes sense."

"Let me make my move or Jie is going to get her hooks in." Apple pulled away, gave Nick a kiss on the cheek and went over to the table where everyone else was sitting. Cale had his thumbs on the sides of his boxers. He had just lost again and was supposed to remove them.

Apple, grabbed Cale's stomach, halting his action.

"Vesper, Cale is exactly what I want for the night. Put it on tab and I'll come in tomorrow and pay when I bring the other girls in with me." Apple knew it meant big money for Vesper if all her friends came with her. She was fairly certain Vesper would give her Cale.

"You can't stay?" Vesper recognized Jie was going to be very angry.

"No." Apple turned her attention to Cale. "Hey lover-boy, get dressed. You're mine and we have to go."

"I gotta go?" Cale asked in wonder.

"Yeah, we've got to go." Apple was again charmed

by his boyish look and attitude, drunk or not.

Nick smiled. He owed Apple big time. He wondered what she was like in bed watching her help Cale get dressed. She was very sexy.

Jie protested in Chinese, but Vesper ignored her. The money Apple spent and the ladies that came with her, far outweighed anything Jie could offer for this one night. Ironic. She hadn't even considered Apple buying Cale. It ruined her plan of teaching Cale and Nick a lesson.

Nick went over to Apple and Cale.

"Looks like you are out of here." Nick said smiling.

Cale nodded, "Yeah, gotta go." He knew he was wasted.

"You kids have a good time." Nick winked at Apple.

She smiled, "Oh we will." Taking Cale's hand they headed to the door.

Vesper looked at Nick after the couple had left. "Do you want to play?"

Nick shook his head. "Nah, I'm no good at games."

Vesper wasn't stupid. She knew somehow Nick put the idea of buying Cale into Apple's head. She could tell from the smile on his face. He had messed with one of her goals, again. She had intended for Cale to have an unpleasant experience. She hadn't counted on Nick watching out for Cale. This wasn't such a good turn of events.

"I think you are very good at games. Being too good almost makes one forget they are like everybody else."

"You are being way too Zen for me now." Nick lit a cigarette.

"Sit down and play." Nick was starting to make her a little angry.

"I don't want to play this game. I know I'm supposed to be with Violet tonight; why not get this all over with?" Nick exhaled smoke.

"I thought Cale would be with Jie tonight so maybe.." Vesper knew this conversation was really going to antagonize him.

Nick cut her off, "Didn't happen that way, huh?" Nick took another drag.

"Maybe…" She was cut off again.

"Violet. Don't you think it's about time we had our fun tonight?"

Vesper turned and gave him a long cold stare, "Maybe, I'm going to buy you out and Jie can come along." Vesper knew it was drunkenness speaking.

Violet started to say something. She had specifically requested Nick at the beginning of the evening, and had given Vesper the money in advance to buy him out.

"Vesper, you know that it isn't going to happen." Nick smiled and put out the cigarette in the ashtray. "Come on Violet. I've been waiting all night to have you in my arms." He said it to get a larger tip, because she did tip well, and also to needle Vesper who was obviously getting angry.

Jie interrupted. "I am going to Zaga. This is all bullshit." She was furious that Cale had left and Nick was leaving with Violet.

"The only bullshit I know is what you do in bed." Nick knew she understood his meaning. Jie was an excellent English speaker, almost as good as Apple or Vesper.

"You were well paid." Jie retorted back angrily.

"Not enough for your idea of fun." Nick looked straight into Jie's face. The age lines were showing around the once beautiful eyes.

"Vesper," Jie started. She was going to start speaking in rapid fire Chinese and tell her to punish Nick for his rudeness.

"Jie, you are a good friend and I try and make you happy." Vesper purposely kept in English so Nick would understand completely. "You have gone too far with some of my employees and they were not pleased. I think maybe tonight you would be better off in Zaga." Vesper gave a sweet smile. She didn't like this confrontation, but Nick had forced it on her, so it was smarter to look like she cared about her workers. She was very angry with Nick. This night had gone completely wrong.

Jie was incensed and a torrent of cursing accompanied her departure.

"Am I still needed here or can we go?" Nick asked nicely.

"Yes go. Something tells me you are going to need money tomorrow." Vesper was going to accuse him of telling Apple to buy Cale but thought better of it in front of Violet.

"O.K.," Nick said grabbing his nearby coat.

"Nick, I really don't like this." Vesper brushed back her hair. She looked directly at him.

"I think you brought all this on yourself, Vesper. Maybe you should lose the dragon lady persona. It makes you seem old and desperate." Nick opened the door. Violet exited quickly. She could tell Nick and Vesper were on the verge of a fight.

"I can make you..." Vesper stopped herself. She knew she was drunk and saying anything in anger to Nick would make her look stupid. But he was pushing her buttons.

"I'll take your advice, Nick. I don't want to appear old or especially desperate. Have a good night." She smiled as the door closed. Reaching down she picked up a whiskey glass and threw it at the floor, hard. Vesper went and turned the stereo off.

CHAPTER 13

The Next Morning

Cale awoke in his underwear, in a strange bed. The smell in the room had traces of perfume bouquet. He heard the shower running in the en suite.

"Jesus," he thought to himself. That drinking game had sent him flying. Cale remembered leaving with Apple. "Did I have sex with her?" He thought to himself as he lay in bed waiting for her to come back. At least he hoped it was her. He really couldn't remember anything past getting into a taxi at Vesper's place.

Apple turned off the water. She wondered if her sleeping prince was up. Last night he had been very cute as she helped him undress. She had gotten his shirt off and was unbuckling his pants when he told her she was beautiful.

"Thanks, Cale." She said taking the compliment with a smile. "Lift up." Apple instructed as she pulled off his trousers. Cale was left in his underwear. Tight boxers. She liked the look.

"No, I mean…ever since I saw you the first time I thought you were just beautiful." Cale repeated. Then he said, "You're nice too."

She stood up and kissed his forehead. Apple toyed with starting something hot, but her instincts told her to wait.

"Are we supposed to have sex?" Cale looked into her brown eyes.

"No." Apple smiled. "Time for bed. I'm up early and I think you could use the rest."

"Really?" Cale lay on the bed and passed out immediately.

Apple looked over the body sleeping on her bed. She smiled and said quietly, "Another day Cale."

The water ran hot and she came back to the present. She bundled herself in a plush rose-colored cotton robe. Apple walked into the bedroom. She saw he was awake and said, "Hey you're up."

"Yeah, I guess so." Cale stayed under the covers.

"Sorry, to rush you, but I've got to be out the door in twenty minutes." She kept her voice low.

"I'm never drinking again." Cale put his hands on his head. Actually he didn't feel all that bad, but his loss of memory made him feel vulnerable.

Apple smiled and said, "Maybe it's just smarter not to get involved in Chinese drinking games with women who have been playing for years."

Cale nodded. Then he looked down at his bare chest.

"I don't remember last night." He wanted to ask if they had been together sexually, but he doubted it. Cale didn't think he'd forget having sex with her. Plus he was in his underwear. Usually when they came off, they stayed off until the next morning. He looked at Apple.

"That's why Nick had me buy you." Apple smiled. She wanted him to know the truth, but this was fun.

Cale was totally taken aback. "Nick?!"

Apple noticed the stubble growing on his face. She liked it. It reminded her of men she knew back in Toronto.

"Yeah, Nick." She patted his leg hidden under the covers. "Nick claimed you were about to be sold to a shark. A lady who likes to cause pain and sometimes leaves scars."

"And Nick had you buy me?"

"Yes."

"Wow." Cale was feeling grateful to his friend.

"Yes, actually it is wow. Nick was doing something for someone without benefit to himself." Apple laughed a little.

Cale came to Nick's defense. "Apple, he is not as self serving as you are making him out to be. He's been a good friend to me since the day I came to this city."

"That is great Cale, but before you came along, Nick showed few human qualities." She laughed a little as she saw Cale frown. Apple then said, "I'm just kidding. Nick has always been fun to be around. He's sexy, great to look at and very smart. He is also a little cold. But it all works for him. He even has Vesper a little in love with him. Then, last night, I saw Nick watch out for a friend. It was nice to see. Really."

"I guess Nick does watch out for me." Cale wasn't sure what to make of the information about Vesper being in love with Nick.

"Do you need watching over?"

Cale smiled at her and stretched his body. "Yeah, I probably do. I've done some things... well, I wouldn't know where to start or how to explain."

"That's O.K., I've had a very different road since I left my folk's place in North York."

"North York, Ontario?" Cale knew the area around Toronto from when he visited his cousin.

"Most of my life. I've only lived in Taiwan for a little over three years."

Cale stretched again and let out a little yawn, "That's interesting. I have a cousin that used to live downtown. Now he's stationed in some African country."

Apple laughed and lightly slapped his exposed chest. "If it's so interesting, then why are you yawning?"

Cale shook his head. "Sorry. Guess I'm still waking up. What brought you to Taiwan?'

"Grandmother. She needs someone to live with her. You know, make sure she is O.K. It is a granddaughter's duty." Apple added quietly, "Besides I wanted to get out of Canada for a while."

"Why?" Cale sat up a bit.

She sighed, "School wasn't going so well. I needed to get my head together."

"What were you studying?" Cale was relieved it wasn't because she had sworn fidelity to her grandmother. The thought of Helena's grandmother still freaked him out.

"I was getting my masters in International Relations."

"Impressive."

"Not really. It seems like all good Chinese girls in North York study IR or go into law. The real go getters try for their MBA."

"Still, impressive." Cale smiled at her. She was

beautiful, freshly showered without any makeup.

"Not so impressive if you are doing badly."

"Difficult?"

"Bad break-up equals bad grades."

"Ending relationships isn't easy." Cale's voice got quieter.

"You're a man with a lot of breakups?"

"I don't know how to answer that question. Too many loose ends."

"But she is dead. Your girlfriend was killed by a bomb."

Cale held in his surprise she knew of Helena's death. He wanted to ask how, but guessed that Vesper had let many of her customers know about the new guy.

He spoke softly, "Yes and we had a big fight just before she died. I said some things I wish I hadn't." Cale's eyes got misty. "I know at least one person who thinks I'm responsible for her death." Helena's grandmother came to mind again.

Apple was on the bed moving a little closer to Cale's body. "I think as long as you know you weren't responsible, other's thoughts are not worth listening to."

"I think if the fight hadn't happened, she wouldn't have gone to the club…" Cale's voice trailed off.

"If you hadn't gone on holiday, if you hadn't stayed at that hotel, if you hadn't tied your shoelaces up. You can't change what happened."

"I can't help blaming myself a little. It's just how it is."

"Then Cale why are you in Taiwan doing what you are doing?"

Cale rolled over a little to face Apple better. "It's a holding pattern for me. I know it sounds crazy, but I need to be a different person."

"Holding pattern?" Apple adjusted the sash on her robe as she made herself more comfortable on the bed.

"Apple I really don't know what I want to do with my life right now." Cale sighed. He put the palms of his hands to his eyes. "I should probably go back to Australia and finish school, but I'm not sure Australia is the place for me."

"What are you studying?"

"Marine biology."

"No kidding?" Apple smiled at him.

"No kidding." Cale flexed his body.

"Masters?"

"Does it show? How come you didn't say PhD?"

"You don't walk out on PhD programs."

"Yeah, I guess that's true."

"So after the bombing, you are on hold. That makes sense." Apple said with candor.

"Hope so. What about you?"

Apple looked at Cale's thigh sticking out from the covers and found herself wanting to stroke it. Instead she said, "Cale sorry, I told you, I have to run." She stood up. "My life story is way longer than five minutes and that is all we have."

"Do I have time for a shower?" Cale asked moving up a little disappointed their morning was ending.

"If you can be really fast, but I have a class and I can't be late."

Cale rubbed his chest. "It's O.K. I'll grab one when I get home."

"Your clothes are on that chair over there." Apple pointed and rolled off the bed. She walked to the bathroom.

Cale dressed quickly. He said goodbye with a wave at her reflection in the bathroom door and let himself out. Cale found a taxi.

Fifteen minutes later, he was in the apartment. Cale put his keys on the desk by the front door when his cell phone rang. It was Nick.

"Hey Cale, you alive?"

"I've felt better." Cale laughed a little.

"What are you doing?"

"Heading off to the shower to wash off last night's evil doings."

"Hold off and we can shoot over to the spa, if you are up for it, my treat. Violet and I are getting ready to leave her place."

"Didn't you spend enough money on me last night?"

"Well yeah. That's why I want to get together. We need a buddy talk. Vesper set last night up for some reason. And I can't say for sure what the reason is. Yet. Let's hit the spa … unless you are too worn out from Apple. But I doubt that."

"What makes you so sure?' Cale was laughing now.

"Because it would have been the first thing you said to me."

"You haven't let me say much."

"O.K. Tell me. What happened?"

"We'll talk at the spa. But it's my treat to say thanks for looking out for me last night."

"Cool. I'll bring along a little attitude adjustment

we can smoke before going in. I never smoked what I took along last night."

"Great. Let's meet at the front door in forty-five minutes."

"See you there." Nick hung up.

Cale went to the bathroom and washed his face. The game plan for the day was a good one. His mind drifted to Apple and how sexy she had been in her robe. He stopped himself and looked into his shaving mirror. A little smile crept across his face as he thought to himself.

I'm going to need a special massage if I keep thinking about Apple this way.

CHAPTER 14

Seven Weeks Later

Cale was blown away watching Nick dance. He had a style that had evolved into a form of improvisation that reacted to the rhythm of the crowd around him as much as the rhythm of the music. The song was another house anthem he'd heard at clubs since the year two thousand; it was stale. But as Nick moved to it he took over the room.

Women and men alike were watching him with the kind of spellbound look usually reserved for the theater. Nick was above professional; he moved throughout the dance floor like a satyr.

Cale and Nick had gone out many times before to Taiwanese dance clubs. Although Cale had noted Nick had danced well, this was special. Something he had been saving.

Women, front and back, were trying to dance off of him, daring themselves and each other to gain his attention. Nick entertained every one of the different women as though it was their own private party, for a moment. Then without losing the beat, swept another brave female off of her feet in one long unending spin before setting her down again to swoon and laugh with her friends.

Before the song was done, two female dancers gyrating on top of two large platforms got down together and invited Nick to dance alone above the crowd. He jumped up.

Nick remembered the last time he had let himself go like this. It had been in Vegas, the night Vesper met him.

Tonight he really was comfortable, a lot of it due to Cale. He had to admit he owed Vesper.

The next electric moments, Nick showed the people of this place, why he believed in himself as a dancer. The crowd was dazed; they had never seen such an Apollo in the flesh – that could dance. Really dance.

Cale saw a couple of girls. They started screaming and crying out of joy and excitement as Nick slid his hands down his legs while gyrating his hips slightly in perfect time with the beat. His biceps gleamed in the club lighting.

"Wow," Cale muttered as Nick got off the stage. A mob surrounded his friend. Nick smiled. He didn't seem uncomfortable with the attention.

"Nick's got it made." Cale said as a few models pressed themselves into a mob around him.

Cale opted to walk over to where Nick was now cornering the latest popular model, Liv Laoung. Cale had seen her in the magazines and newspapers - she was a definite media darling.

"Hey." Nick said as he got next to Cale.

Cale spontaneously grabbed Nick and hugged him. "No wonder you got Vesper's attention with your dancing. You were fucking awesome."

"Well, you just better be careful, I think you have her attention now." They both laughed. Nick turned and introduced Cale to Liv. A couple more people Liv knew made their way into the conversation.

Nick gave Liv a kiss and said, "My friend and I are going over to La Bodega for a drink, hope I see you there."

Liv nodded and smiled.

Nick turned to Cale,

"Let's blow this place."

"What? No encore?"

"No, legends are made this way." Nick laughed. They went outside.

"Let's walk." Said Nick as they went to the street. "La Bodega is only twenty minutes away on foot."

There were people emptying out with them. The club, KK had been a factory for ceramics in earlier days. The club was permitted a crowd of two thousand. It was located off a main street and had taxis lined up along the curb, waiting for fares. There were plenty of customers.

"It will take longer than that." Cale smiled knowing Nick had an ulterior motive.

"We can cab it." Nick looked at the line of taxis.

"No, I'm kidding, it's a great night out." Cale turned to his right.

"I think Liv is a possibility tonight." Nick said moving away from the front entrance of KK.

"No shit. Dude, anyone who saw you ten minutes ago is in awe."

"In awe? Really?" Nick chuckled.

"Come on. You know you rocked everyone." Cale stopped and faced Nick, who also halted. "I'm a believer now. Nick Young is a dancer."

"Thanks." Nick said feeling warm. It felt great to have a friend.

Cale questioned, "I bet you got a joint, don't you? That's part of the reason for the stroll, isn't it?"

"Am I that easy to read?" Nick pulled out a rolled cigarette. He gave it to Cale.

As he lit it, Cale looked around. All was safe. This far away from the club the streets were empty. He took two drags and handed it over to Nick. Cale exhaled.

"I can't believe I'm a male-whore pot-head in Taiwan."

Nick choked a little, laughing. He handed the burning joint to Cale, "All you have to say is no." Nick said pulling out his knife to inspect the blade.

"Yeah, no shit." Cale took one more hit. "It's almost cashed."

"I love I'm living in Taiwan, a male – whore, who just smoked a joint."

Cale looked at Nick's knife changing the subject. "You keep that pretty close."

Nick looked up at Cale. "Ya keeping a knife is a bit of a legacy thing."

"Huh? Legacy?"

"Let's get moving." Nick threw the roach on the ground and stamped it out silently. "I've been handy with the knife since I was little over eight." Nick folded the knife and handed it to Cale.

"Eight? You're not serious?"

"Ya, my brothers had me talking about arteries, veins and tissue density from a young age." Nick laughed, "You know the standard New York City education."

As they approached a busy intersection, Cale handed the knife back to Nick and said, "Yeah, well, I missed out, and I'm glad."

Nick looked at the ground, "I miss the Twin Towers."

Cale looked down too as they maneuvered around sidewalk stalls and an endless stream of people as the came to Shi Tun Lu, a major street in the city. It got busier after 10 PM with all the night market stalls that appeared once the day businesses closed.

"What do you mean? The World Trade Center?"

"No. No. My brothers. My big brothers."

"Why did you call them the 'Twin Towers'?"

"Lots of reasons. For starters, they are both six-foot-six."

"No way. What happened to you?"

"I was sort of the milkman's baby. We don't look anything alike."

"Are they back in New York?"

"Yeah, if lockdown counts." Nick looked down to the ground again.

"Jail?"

"I told you this when we first met."

"O.K., but you didn't go into much detail."

"Well, they were always getting into trouble. It was almost like competition." Nick gave a little chuckle.

"What are they in for?"

"Evening the score on what some assholes did to me." Nick's voice was quieter as they moved off Shi Tun Lu, to a smaller street that would take them to their final destination.

Cale stopped. "Can I ask what happened?"

Nick stopped too. "Sure. You are about the only

person I'm going to talk to about it."

"Seems like I only talk to you about my life." Both looked each in the eye, neither one uncomfortable. "It's cool."

"Yeah, it is."

"So what happened?" Cale went back to the subject.

"Well to start with, believe it or not, they stuck an ice pick through my foster father's nut sack." Nick gave a little chuckle.

"Wow."

"My brothers didn't always sit on the right side of the law, but when it came to protecting me, they were golden. Plus, they really taught me how to use a knife." Nick hugged his arms around his chest as his tone got lower. "The Twin Towers got wind of me getting abused on their first day out of jail." Nick cleared his throat and continued, "They gave my foster dad an anatomy lesson."

"But they didn't kill him? Just the ice pick in sack?"

"Well they didn't kill him that time. Just scared the fuck out of him."

"What do you mean?"

"My foster mother caused it all to get out of hand." Nick shook his head, almost unaware of Cale's last words. "She was a real winner."

"Why do you say that?" Cale was trying to follow Nick's story, but it was becoming difficult.

"Oh I don't know. What do you say about a fat bitch who likes to fuck her foster sons?" There was heavy sarcasm in Nick's voice.

"No way!" Cale stopped.

Nick stopped too. He faced Cale. "You must really

be a good friend and I must be pretty stoned or I'd never talk about this shit."

"You don't have to talk about any of this. I'd understand." Cale's voice was quiet, but loud enough to be heard on the small, deserted street they were on.

"You have trusted me a few times." Nick moved a little closer to where Cale was standing and lit a cigarette.

Cale watched the red ember glowing in the dark.

"Her name was Polly." Nick took a deep drag. Exhaling he said, "Huge tits." Nick laughed a little.

Cale laughed along with his friend. The tension was broken.

"Anyway, she was sorta cool the first few weeks I lived with them." Nick took another drag and then continued, "Then one time she comes in while I'm taking a shower."

"You left the door unlocked?"

"Wasn't allowed to lock doors. Not really an outrageous rule if you think about having foster kids who are considered a bit troubled."

"You were considered troubled?"

"No, I was considered just plain trouble. Anyway you want to hear about this or not. My train of thought is somewhat compromised right now."

"Sure, sure. Sorry. How old were you?"

Nick took another drag. "Fifteen."

"Had you had sex yet?" Cale looked at the nearby lamp. A cloud of insects hovered in the light.

"A few times. A couple older girls."

"You were destined to be a stud." Cale said with humor.

Nick laughed. Then he said, "Blew-up in my face that time."

"So what happened?"

"Well she comes in telling me she has to check me for crabs."

"Crabs?"

"Yeah, she said the last kid had crabs and she wasn't taking any chances. She also said she knew where to look." Nick took another drag and said, "My dick and balls were given a working over."

"Guess you couldn't really say much."

"Say what? I told her I didn't have them but I had nurses seen me naked before, so I was like sure, go ahead. Besides, I was still a kid and she was an adult authority figure."

"Still, having your foster mother looking you over had to be strange. "

"Well, ya, it was. The next thing, she's getting me hard and I'm asking her to stop." Nick sighed. "We had a small battle and she left the bathroom. The next thing I know foster dad starts hitting me for any little thing." Nick rubbed his forehead and said, "The Twin Towers had just gotten out of the slam that week. They saw me a bit bruised and went ballistic." Nick put out his cigarette. "What happened to the guy's nut sack, I only know because of the trial." Nick smiled. "They did know their shit when it came to cutting up the body."

"So he didn't turn them in?" Cale asked rubbing his neck.

"No he was cowered into keeping quiet, but good old Polly used the whole scene to her advantage."

"How so?"

The streetlight they had stopped under cast shadows on Nick's face. There was a half-minute of silence. Nick looked at Cale in the eyes and said, "Polly met me at school because I was living with my brothers by then. She told me to meet her at this old motel outside of the neighborhood."

"And you went?" That definitely didn't seem like a smart move to Cale no matter what age Nick was.

"Of course, once she said she'd go to the police and tell them about my brothers and what they did to her husband." Nick looked down on the ground. "I wasn't stupid and knew she was going to try and break me somehow, but I had to go for my brothers." He looked from the ground to the dark sky. There were no stars shining there.

"And you were fifteen?"

"Ya, I was." Nick looked from the sky directly into Cale's eyes through the darkness. "She did a lot of things to me that were pretty fucked-up." He rubbed his head.

"Let's sit down over there. I see a couple chairs." Cale said observing three plastic chairs people left out to sit near water, although the canal was actually a large sewer.

Across from the water was a high school so the street was deserted at this time of night.

"Might have to light-up another joint."

"Might have to."

Cale and Nick moved across the street and sat down in the chairs. Nick lit the hash cigarette. He took three quick drags and handed it to Cale.

Taking the smoking joint from Nick, Cale asked, "Do you want to tell any of the stuff she did?"

"It would be easier telling you what she didn't do."

Nick watched Cale exhale and took the hand rolled cigarette from his friend. Taking just one hit and exhaling, Nick said, "Handcuffs, whip and blindfold." His voice trailed off, "It was pretty sick."

"That sucks, Nick." Cale said looking over at his friend.

Nick looked back at Cale and handed him the joint. "You had plenty on your plate at fifteen."

Cale took a hit and exhaled. "Yeah, it was not a good year, in fact, you're right, it was terrible. But it didn't involve handcuffs."

"That wasn't the worst Cale. She brought her fucking dildo." Nick looked down to his feet.

Cale shut his eyes. His voice was almost a whisper, "No."

"She tore me up every which way bro."

"What did you do?"

"I didn't have to do much, except go home."

"What do you mean?"

"Cale, the woman used a whip all over my ass and dick. Plus I had a few bruises from the cuffs. It's not like I took it all without putting up a fight."

"Fuck." Cale said lowly. He handed the joint to Nick.

Taking the smoking butt, Nick continued, "Ya, The Twin Towers looked over my body and, and..." Nick gulped. "Well they got me to a clinic, and then they killed Polly and her husband." He took a puff. "Long trial. They got thirty years instead of the death penalty because of what was done to me." Nick blew out the smoke. "Guess you understand why I scooted off to Vegas, soon as I could."

"Jesus."

"Guess it goes without saying, I don't talk about this much." Nick took another hit and handed it to Cale.

"No shit." Cale asked softly, "Were you physically damaged at all?"

"You mean from what she did with all her toys? Might still have a little scar on my shoulder. I'll have you look sometime. The dildo, made me sore as hell for a couple days and doctors probing, was a bit embarrassing, but I got out of it with no long-term damage. A lot of kids get it worse."

"I really don't know how I would cope."

"I did fine because of the Twin Towers. They are the best."

"Do you keep in much contact?"

"Hell yes. A letter to one or the other, every two or three weeks. They've never waited more than a month."

"They write you back?"

"Not as much as me. About once a month I get a letter from one of them."

"They know about your life here?"

"No detail left out."

"Do they have a chance for parole?"

"I don't know. They don't have great track records."

"You ever get arrested?"

"Not really."

"Not really means what?"

"A couple brushes, but nothing to put me in front of court. What about you?"

"No, I was like you. A couple brushes, but nothing serious."

"I'm pretty stoned."

"I'm the lightweight remember?"

"You're doing a decent job of being a contender."

Cale laughed.

Nick smiled and asked, "You still feel like going to La Bodega?"

"Doesn't matter, I'm cool with hanging here a bit."

Nick pulled out his knife. "You know how to really make an effective wound on a man?"

"I think it is possible I'm going to hear very soon."

Nick looked at the shiny blade and said, "You know I haven't even told you my brothers' names." His voice was low.

"What are they?"

"Don't laugh, but their names are Kane and Abel-Abe for short."

"You're not serious?" Cale couldn't keep the amusement out of his voice. "Those are the brothers where one kill the other. Are your folks religious?"

"My folks? Hardly. Just had a strange sense of humor. At least the spelling for Kane is different."

"Did they ever say why they named your brothers Kane and Abel?" Cale reflected a second or two and said, "I'm not sure your parents did them any favors giving them those names."

Nick laughed. "Of course they did them no favors. My parents are two people of failed dreams. Lying and scheming were the basic rules of their household. Not that we were together all that much."

"God, my family was so different."

"Ya, that comes through bro." Nick looked into

Cale's face, which looked back, "Don't doubt the strong goodness your folks gave you, because there are plenty of us who wish we had been brought up that way."

"Yeah, but sometimes... Well you know the story."

"Cale, there may be a day, I need you the way your friend in Bali needed you. You might say no again, but I'll admire how you search your soul in coming to the answer. I bet your parents are proud of you up in heaven."

"Nick that was very cool of you to say to me."

"The truth is good to hear." Nick lit a cigarette.

"Are your folks still in jail?"

"Last I heard, but that's been a while."

"Why?"

"I'm basically disowned."

"What?"

"We are swimming in deep waters." Nick exhaled smoked and rubbed his head.

"I'm a pretty good swimmer."

Nick smiled as he took another drag. "You are a good friend, Cale." Nick paused as he exhaled. "It must've killed you to say no to your friend in Bali."

Cale took a deep breath. "Sure it did. I think you are the only person to really get it."

"Who else do you need?"

Cale laughed a little. "Right now, where I am in my life, it is very cool you do understand."

Nick took one last drag and put out his cigarette. He picked up his knife. "The reason my father disliked me, I truly was a milkman's baby. His reasons for not being loving are obvious."

"Wow. What about your mother?"

"She was way worse. From my earliest memories, nothing I did was ever good enough. I think it is because my real father disappeared right before I was born. I never even got to meet the guy."

"That sucks."

"Ya, I guess so." Nick looked at his knife. "Kane and Abe saved me. They're my heroes. They did everything in their power to protect me and show me how to protect myself." He laughed. "Those guys were so excellent. Both kept my education on the ways of life fairly advanced."

"Huh, what do you mean?"

"Uhm… hey, what time is it?"

"Almost 11:30." Cale said looking at his watch.

"Let's get moving. Liv might be at La Bodega right now." Nick stood up putting his knife away.

Cale stood up also and brushed the back of his pants with his hands. He got his cell out. "Probably should give Brian a call. Think your night is already in motion with Liv." Cale looked for the number as he said, "Haven't hung out with him for a while and he's called me a couple times this past month."

"Don't call him, I don't need to meet up with Liv."

"What are you talking about?" Cale looked from his phone to Nick.

"I don't really want him around tonight." Nick looked to the ground.

"You really don't like him," Cale said putting his cell back in his front pocket.

"No, I don't."

"I don't get it. He's a decent guy."

"Ya, well, guess we just aren't cut from the same cloth."

"Are we?" Cale said looking at his friend.

Nick smiled. "Maybe not exactly the same cloth, but fabric is almost woven the same."

Cale laughed. "That's clever Nick."

"Ya, well, I'm stoned so I'm more witty right now."

"You're smart all the time."

"Ya, but not educated smart like you and Brian."

"Ahh… do I detect a little academic insecurity? Could that be why you don't like Brian?"

"That's really not fair Cale. I'm schooled about a lot of things and some things no. When I'm around Brian, it's like he's out to act superior because he's a college guy."

Cale looked down the street. It was completely empty. Then he spoke, "I'm not defending him, but don't you think you act the same way to him?"

"What do you mean?" Nick felt himself getting defensive.

"Look, Brian is good looking enough, but you have a cover boy face with a body that can dance like a motherfucker. You have women like Liv Laoung, waiting for you on nights like this and on top of it you get paid for sex." Cale rubbed the back of his head. "Bro, you're a tough guy to get to know and it comes across loud and clear." Cale took a breath and continued, "I know I'm lucky to have you as my friend. You have helped me in so many ways. Since my folks died, there hasn't been anyone in my life I feel I can be so open with. Not even my cousin Jace or Helena." Cale's voice got lower. "But dude, you are hard to approach. I see it all the time. You blow people off without giving it any thought. I'm not sure you can use this excuse Brian acts superior to you and you don't like him for it."

Nick shook his head. "I must be stoned, because I'm actually listening to you."

"I think that is why we are alike."

"What do you mean?"

"I gotta be really stoned before I listen to you." Cale laughed out loud.

Nick made a mock punch at Cale's face.

Both laughed a little harder as they messed around giving each other playful taps.

Cale threw up his arms in fake surrender. "O.K. you're the victor. I give up."

Nick gave him a light slap on his cheek. "You're no fun."

"Nick, chill on your dislike for Brian. He doesn't go out of his way to say anything bad about you." Cale lowered his voice as he said honestly to his friend, "It gets old you never wanting to be around him. And Jesus, if you are, you act like you could care less what he has to say."

"It isn't an act."

Cale smiled. "O.K., no Brian tonight. But do me a favor and give the guy a chance. He's my friend and he is pretty cool."

"Sure, sure. Your point is taken. A new generous Nick is born. To prove it, I'll share Liv tonight."

"Share? What are you talking about?"

"We'll snag her and maybe a friend or two of hers if they are still hanging around. Give them a good time." Nick had a big grin.

"What are you talking about?' Cale was lost.

"Hey, I'm not the only good-looking guy here who gets paid to have sex. Getting the two of us in the same bed with the ladies should be easy." Nick smiled again as he said, "Good training for when Apple buys us out together."

Cale's voice got louder, "What are you talking about?"

Nick kept his smile. "Rumor has it, Apple is going to buy us both one night soon. The world will be anxiously awaiting the show we are going to give." Nick laughed.

"You're kidding."

"Nope. It's not really a rumor. Vesper told me. She doesn't want a repeat of our last buyout together."

"I thought you talked to Vesper and she understood I'm not into gay shit."

"You also said you'd do anything if Apple bought us out. Only reason I agreed to this. Those were your words."

"No…" Cale shook his head. "Jesus Nick, I'm not ready for that."

Nick came closer and patted Cale's shoulder. "Don't sweat the little stuff. The point is, Apple is buying us. I don't think it is because she wants to see us fuck around. I think she wants to fuck around with us."

"So why is Vesper even telling you any of this?"

Nick started to walk away. " You caused a scene man that is legendary in the world of Escapade. She wants to make sure it doesn't happen again. And we don't need to be on Vesper's bad side. No more Jie encounters."

"Because I didn't want a goddamn blow job from you, she's this spiteful?" Cale came up to his side.

"Don't be so sure of that blowjob buddy. That was no sure thing. However, you made us a target by your unwillingness to let the ladies have their fun. Now it's made us expensive, so I guess that is good. However, Vesper knows she looks bad every time she refuses a customer our joint services. It's a face thing man. Apple is the right choice for this to all happen and make it right for everyone."

"I should have never said those words when we got high. This sucks."

"You or me?" Nick laughed and punched him gently.

"Stop it Nick. I'm not kidding. Call me a redneck, but I'm dead set against this whole scene."

"Guess, this means we better stop and have another joint."

"How many did you roll?"

Nick laughed. "A few."

Both stayed silent as Nick sparked up the cigarette.

After taking a couple tokes, Nick handed it to Cale. They were in a small alley that was completely deserted.

"Cale, look at it as acting."

"I'm not an actor and have no desire to be one." Cale took a drag and another, back to back and gave the joint to Nick. As he exhaled he said, "Nick I love you as a brother, but this is not in me."

Nick looked down at the ground and said in a quiet voice, "Like I said before, Apple is not the first to offer to buy us. I'm positive it is the whole reason the night with Jie happened. Vesper was getting even in her own way."

"She wanted to punish me?"

"Yeah, but it backfired." Nick looked up at Cale and laughed.

"What a fucking bitch."

"No she isn't. She just can't have work rules being

ignored by her wei gor rens. Bad for business."

"You mean us?"

"Yeah. All the other workers know what the customer wants, she gets. I've tested Vesper's authority a few times on this point before you came along. I'm sure she regrets like hell she had me meet you that day in Fashion Cafe."

Cale saw Vesper's dilemma. "Well I can quit."

"Sure you can. Do you want to?"

Cale looked at his friend. He shook his head. "Not really."

"Why?"

Cale smiled, "Because Apple might buy me again."

"You can ask her out." Nick put out the joint.

"No, I can't. It's going to sound weird, but if women weren't buying me, I don't think I'd have been with any women for the past six months."

"Not counting prostitutes?"

Cale smiled. "O.K., you got me."

"Nah, I understand what you are talking about." Nick sighed slightly. "Better than you think."

"That sounds like you got something to tell me." Cale often wondered about Nick's life. He was closed about most of his past even though he professed his openness to Cale.

"Ya. I told Vesper, if Apple bought us together, it could solve her problem."

Cale realized Nick was ignoring his last comment.

"It doesn't look like she is controlled by her two white boys and we get to fuck a beauty." Nick rubbed his eye as he finished speaking.

"What if she doesn't let us fuck her? And bro, what

if she wants a show like those other ladies did?"

"I don't think she will." Nick came up close, "If she does, we'll give it to her."

"You are so full of shit." Cale put his hands to his head. "I can't believe this is happening."

"You're going to thank me later."

"I don't know about that."

"Cale, I'm not going to do anything with you that you can't handle. I get where you are coming from. But you've come a long ways since the guy I met at High Fashion Café." Nick's voice got softer, "Plus I see how you and Apple look at each other. You both seem to be in the same place. One thing though, she's not going to buy you out solo again. Just think of me as the icebreaker."

Cale let out a loud sigh. "Fuck."

Nick moved away. "Cale I'm not any... fuck what's the word where you know everything in the future and tell people?"

"Prophet?"

"Ya prophet." Nick faced his friend and cleared his throat. "You tell me things, I listen. You listen to me. We are supposed to be in each other's lives."

Cale smiled. "You are stoned aren't you?"

Nick admitted to himself he was feeling exceptionally open. "Am I getting bad?"

Cale kept his smile and shook his head. "No, anything but. If you see me and Apple getting together this way, then I trust you. Just remember uh..." Cale wasn't sure how he was going to finish his sentence.

"That you are not comfortable with threesomes. That's why I thought we'd get some practice in tonight."

"Huh?! You are serious."

"As a heart attack. I'd use a whore, but Liv and company seem way more challenging." Nick chuckled. " Remember, Apple and you might have some attraction going, but she is still paying and who knows what she will want. You can't be farm boy Cale."

"I think she likes farm boy Cale."

"No doubt." Nick smiled again. "Let's just see what we can get going with Liv and her friends."

"Group sex?"

"Dude, we're industry experts. We should be doing stuff like this once a week."

"You really are unbelievable."

"Let's make a bet who can make the woman moan loudest. It will be fun."

"No way." Cale couldn't help laughing.

"The loser has to buy the next spa time including special massage."

"A sex competition."

"Ya. Might as well throw a little competition in our life. Like if we were playing basketball one on one."

"I think there is a reason you don't have a lot of friends." Cale was laughing harder.

"That might be true, but I have you. Means Liv and maybe a friend or two are going to have fun tonight."

"You have a pretty high opinion of yourself." Cale looked down the still deserted alley.

"You just noticed?"

Cale looked down to the ground, but kept his smile. "I don't know about all this."

"Cale the Twin Towers did stuff like this all the time.

Fucking ladies together was more the norm than not." Nick got a small grin. "In fact they were in the room watching me get my first blowjob. I even watched them fuck her when she was done with me."

"No way!" Cale looked up. "I'm not so sure that is so cool Nick. I know you must've been pretty young."

Nick lost his smile and said with a growl in his voice. "Cale they are my brothers. You've never had a blood brother so don't stand there telling me what is right and not concerning them. Everything that happened that day, was done because they love me."

"O.K. Nick. You're right. I don't have the brother thing wrapped under my belt, but I've told you my cousin and I were close when I lived in Canada. We went to strip joints sometimes, but nothing like what you are talking about. So I think I can say, family or not, it seems very intense."

"Thank God it was. That's how they taught me. Told you, my carnal knowledge comes directly from those two. It was natural they would be there for my first blowjob."

"I guess."

"You want to hear the story?"

Cale looked at Nick. His friend had a serious look on his face. "Sure I do." Tonight Nick was divulging more than he ever had, so Cale wanted to hear as much as his friend was going to tell.

"The woman was like us. She got paid when she had sex. She was also a friend of my brothers." Nick lit a cigarette, took a drag and said, " She liked to do them at the same time and they were always game. It was a twin thing."

"No shit."

"No shit. Anyway, I just happened to be there when she came over. Her name was Marla Jensen." Nick laughed, "Don't know why I told you her name."

"Did she charge?"

"My brothers! Hell no. Me, nah."

"How old were you again?"

"Thirteen, maybe fourteen."

"Your brothers were there, watching?"

"Dude, they were cheering me on."

"You know that is against the law."

"Oh ya, the legal system and I are real buddies."

"Still you were too young. That's why it is illegal. Your brothers should have known better." Cale couldn't believe Nick didn't see why it was wrong.

"Cale, don't stand in judgment of my brothers. I can handle it when you stand in judgment of me. You've heard enough to know my brothers love me and would never do anything to harm me." Nick's voice was strong. "I'm not going to even listen to any shit you say about them. In my book they can do no wrong."

"But Nick you were just a kid."

"I was a kid that lived in a world where the rules didn't apply. My brothers knew this. They would have kicked my ass if I didn't use a rubber, but they were all for me to know about sex soon as I wanted to know. That's how they taught me about knives. Know as much as you can and be careful."

Cale stayed quiet for a moment. There was silence between the two. Then Cale said, "You're right. You tell me it was cool, then I know it was."

Nick nodded. He was glad he had made Cale understand. "Thanks, bro."

"So you got a blowjob."

"One of the best." Nick looked at Cale. "How old were you when you got your first?"

Cale remembered back to Randy. "Fifteen."

"And you were giving me shit?"

"I said I was sorry." Cale was getting a little sad remembering his conversation with his father.

"What's wrong?" Nick noticed the change in Cale's voice.

Cale looked up at Nick. "My Dad found out about it. Gave me the father/son lecture on being careful and always telling the truth."

"Well of course he did." Nick laughed.

"He and my mother were killed an hour later."

"Fuck, Cale."

"It's why I can't lie Nick. I promised my father I wouldn't ever lie again and that was the last conversation I had with him."

Nick nodded, but stayed silent.

"I can't make people understand."

"You made me." Nick said quietly.

"O.K., cool."

"Let's get back to the original plan. Liv and company." Nick looked at his watch and then to his friend. He saw Cale's questioning look. He gave Cale a little shove. "You still nervous about us doing this group thing?"

In truth Cale was. "Maybe a little." He gave his friend a shy smile. Then Cale said, "What if she left or didn't show?"

"There is always somebody."

They started to walk in the direction of La Bodega, "You are always so sure."

"My cell phone is filled with sure things. Yours will be soon enough."

"You really are unbelievable." Cale said getting more at ease again.

"No, I'm not. Just being honest. We need a test run before Apple. There are plenty of takers. Just up to us to get the ball rolling." Nick smiled.

"You really are serious about this test run shit."

"I want Apple to be happy. Right now my friend, you are a bit squirrelly about Apple buying us together." Nick paused a second and said, "Makes sense though."

"You've got me stoned enough to where I'm listening."

"I guess sometimes it must be hard to trust me."

"You're wrong. The opposite. You have saved me from myself a few times since I met you."

Nick nodded and smiled. "Ya, maybe. But then again, you wouldn't be in this position right now."

"What position is that?"

"Having to prepare for a group scene with Apple. I told Vesper you'd be cool."

Now Cale smiled. "Nick I'm not going to need a test run to be with Apple. Trust me on that one. I'll do whatever she wants."

"For real?" Nick wasn't convinced, but liked Cale's attitude.

"For real."

"Well, I guess you're off the hook for tonight."

"Who says I want to be? I'd like to get a piece of Liv." Cale laughed at his friend.

CHAPTER 15

Six weeks later Nick and Cale were sitting in the living room of their apartment. It had been nine weeks since Cale and Apple had spent the night together.

"I can't believe you're rolling another." Cale exclaimed. He was feeling lightheaded from all the vodka cranberries he had put down at the bar with Nick.

"No one is forcing you to smoke." Nick said mixing tobacco in with the cannabis he had in a small bowl. He looked up at Cale, smiled, and went back to his job.

Cale nodded. "I know." He looked at his friend. His face was intent on what he was doing. Cale asked a question he had wondered before.

"Nick what was Las Vegas like for you? I remember one night you telling me about when you were hustling, you said that part of your life hardly scratched the surface. What else is there?"

"What?" Nick looked up.

"What was Las Vegas like? You hardly ever mention the place in comparison to New York or Taiwan. I mean, except for Vesper and the little you told me about you being a hustler, I know nothing about your time there."

Nick shook his head. "Maybe nothing interesting happened at that time in my life."

"You put in almost ten years if I got the math right. You were a dancer. It's hard to believe nothing interesting happened. It's just a little strange you never talk about the place."

"There is plenty you don't tell me about growing up in Texas and Canada."

Cale took in his friend's words, then said, "Actually, I told you the other day about the drive I had to the hospital when my parents died. Also told you about a soccer game I played in high school in Canada. Plus tonight, I told you two stories about girls that gave me blowjobs while I was living in Canada. I talk about both places all the time."

Nick finished his job of rolling. He winked at Cale. "Sure you don't want to join me?"

"Tell me about Vegas."

"Jesus, what do you want to know?" Nick lit the joint.

"Something that you haven't told me." Cale licked his lips to moisten them. They felt a little dry.

Nick exhaled and handed the burning cigarette to Cale, who took it without hesitation.

"Any specific subject matter?" Nick looked at his friend.

"I'm not trying to know all that much. But you've got to admit there is a pretty big gap. I'm just curious." Cale took a second drag.

"Why are you so curious?" The joint was back in his possession.

"I don't know." There was a long pause. Both men were now staring at the wall. "Maybe because you don't talk and I know it is missing." Cale gave a small, dry cough, and then continued, "Tonight was fun with you. You had all those ladies around your finger. They were all smoking hot too. It seems pretty natural to ask you about your life in Vegas before you came here."

Nick exhaled smoke. "Maybe you wouldn't like what you hear. A good part of my life was about work and money."

"Yeah. I know all your work here in Taiwan is for charity." Cale laughed.

"It's different. Very different."

"Enlighten me."

"Vegas is two worlds. One is The Strip where it is the place of making your bread and butter." Nick looked down at his hands and said in a quieter voice, "Outside The Strip you have areas like Henderson, where it is mostly a normal city. You know, residential and shopping centers. All surrounded by desert, but nice." Nick looked up at Cale. "Sort of like Phoenix."

"Never been to either place." Cale then asked, "What is The Strip like?"

"A city that has hotels, resorts, nightclubs and restaurants all swirling around casinos." Nick handed the joint to Cale. "It can be a crazy scene because every night is about partying and having a good time."

"So you danced for a living?" Cale held the cigarette without smoking it.

"Ya, I guess you could say that, if you call doing strip shows dancing. Regular gigs were harder to get, but I got those too. Stripping paid way better." Nick let out a small laugh.

"You were a stripper?" Cale laughed back at his friend.

"Ya, a lot of bachelorette and birthday parties. Some special shows here and there."

"In clubs?"

"Sometimes. Private shows are the way to go. Mostly in hotels suites or some private home or condo. Wherever ladies can get together that isn't public."

"Actually sounds cool. Definitely different from what we do here."

"What do you mean?"

"There isn't any stripping at Escapade."

"Bro, you just haven't had the pleasure yet. There are plenty of strip shows for the ladies." Nick got up to get something to drink. He saw Cale put out the joint.

"You want a Pocari Sweat?" Nick asked as he went towards the kitchen. "O.K.," Cale said loudly. "Hey, you aren't trying to change the subject here are you?"

Nick came back with the two cans. "Nah, why would I? It's all about moves and so is dancing."

"What type of moves?" Cale was getting more interested.

"Moves that get women hot." Nick laughed as he sat down. He looked into Cale's eyes.

"I think it's cool." Cale shook his head as he took a drink from his can.

"It's cool in a bar where a girl takes off her shirt or a couple go skinny dipping." Nick had a smile come back to his face as he said, "It's a whole 'nother thing when you're getting paid baby."

Cale burst into laughter.

Nick continued to smile at his friend.

Laughing still, Cale said, "So you led the sordid life of a stripper plus dancing on the side, and you have nothing to talk about as far as Vegas goes?" Cale stopped laughing but said with a big smile, "I don't believe you."

Nick looked at his can. "I don't know how you've done it, but you are going to get me to come clean. Fuck you."

"What are friends for?"

"Ya, I guess. My brothers don't even know the whole story about Martina." Nick let out a sigh.

"Who's Martina?"

"The woman I married." Nick's voice was quiet.

Cale was incredulous. He stuttered his next words. "You, you were married?"

"I was." Nick was still deciding how much he wanted to tell Cale. He thought silently, "It still crushes me."

"Jesus, I had no idea. Does Vesper know?"

"Hell no!" Nick said strongly. "If I'm not telling my brothers much, I'm not telling Vesper anything." He looked down at the ground. "You ready to hear the whole sad story of Nick Young's marriage?"

"Where is she now?" Cale sat up.

"She's dead."

"No way." Cale's mouth dropped open.

"Ya, two years before I left Vegas."

"How?" Cale choked out.

Nick let out a very deep sigh. "She slit her wrists in the bathtub. Classic suicide."

"Why?"

"Fuck Cale, give me a minute." Nick gulped hard.

He tried to steady himself. He didn't want to start bawling in front of Cale. Then he said slowly, "It was a mistake." Nick felt his throat constricting. "She saw something that freaked her out…" His voice went to a whisper, "It involved me and her kid sister."

Cale was at a loss. He could see Nick trembling. His friend's eyes were shut.

"Are you sure you want to talk about this with me?"

Nick opened his eyes.

He saw Cale watching him.

"Ya, well, you know about loss, man. What happened to you was the same thing, different circumstances." Nick's voice got quiet. "It seems right I talk about this with you, 'cause I don't think I can talk about it with anybody else."

"Haven't you spoken to anybody about it?"

"Nah, not really. A grief counselor when it first happened, but I didn't say much. I don't like to talk about it, because I'm still blown away it all happened the way it did. It still kills me."

Cale nodded. It made sense why Nick had been so generous to him when they first met. "You know, you've helped me a lot in dealing with Helena's death."

"Thanks."

"What was your wife's name again?"

"Martina." Nick smiled. "I've never said her name in Taiwan before tonight."

"No kidding?"

"Cale, she killed herself because she was married to me. Nothing much I want to talk about with anyone in this place." Nick took another drink from his can.

"Point taken."

Nick nodded. "Well, I should talk about her. Especially to you. Martina was the greatest woman in my life. No bullshit, Cale."

"O.K. So she was special." Cale kept his voice gentle.

"Ya, well.." Nick's voice trailed off.

"What was she like?"

Nick exhaled deeply. "She made me happy to be alive. Martina loved me tons. I had the best woman in the world for me."

"I believe you."

"Ya, well, believe me it sucked when it all went down."

"Suicide is tough."

Nick took another deep breath. "Too often she thought I was with her out of pity." Nick shut his eyes. Tears were starting to form.

"What do you mean pity?" Cale was as confused by Nick's words as the helplessness he felt seeing tears from his friend. "Why would she think something like that?"

"Martina had some physical deformities that happened at birth and she had been scarred up when she was a little kid in some car accident."

"O.K." The woman Nick was describing had not been the person Cale would have thought his friend would marry. "Are you trying to tell me she wasn't very pretty?"

Nick brushed back his tears. There was edginess to his voice, "What are looks Cale? I'm good-looking so does that mean I'm only supposed to be married to a beautiful woman or it's strange?"

"Don't get mad Nick. It's just that's how it usually

works. Law of attraction."

"Fuck that. I was blown away by Martina the first couple minutes I met her." Nick felt a hot tear run down his left cheek.

"O.K." He was still taking in Nick had cared about a woman deeply. Cale had even felt on occasion Nick that was incapable of caring deeply for any lady. This was a total surprise.

"Guess I've got to tell you the whole story of Nick and Martina, huh?" Nick rubbed his forehead.

"I'm not going anywhere."

Nick smiled slightly. "I met Martina at a gas station on The Strip in Vegas. She was protecting this Arab looking guy from four assholes."

"What do you mean protecting?"

"Martina was always saving the underdog. I guess it was because she understood what it was like to face judgments about her physical appearance."

"Was she really that bad off?" Cale was hesitant to ask about her looks.

"She wasn't ugly, Cale. One leg was shorter so she had this limp. I remember her telling me how she would like to have been able to run across the street like everyone else."

"So you meet at a gas station..."

"Ya. She had some mace that took out a few of the guys and I got in some good solid hits. They were big but they didn't know how to fight."

"She sounds tough."

Nick smiled. "Martina was tough and nobody's fool. I had to beg her for a date."

"I find that hard to believe."

"No it is true. She denied me at first. I had to practically plead." Nick let out a little laugh. "When we finally did go to dinner, she told me she didn't go to bed with anyone for at least six months."

"Guess you got to know her pretty well before…"

Nick interrupted, "Cale, we hooked up the first night."

"The charm of Nick Young strikes!"

"It seemed to just happen naturally. Let me tell you bro, she knocked my socks off in bed. She was the best. Maybe it was because there was love involved, but no woman has really come close to rivaling Martina in bed."

"Love does make it better." Cale said remembering how much he had enjoyed the lovemaking Helena and he had shared.

"It really does." Nick took a sip from his drink.

There was a silence between the two friends for a moment.

"So what happened?"

"Well Martina inspired me to go to school."

"You went to school?" Nick was full of surprises.

"Don't tell anybody. It was for dance, but I still had to take the basic classes. English, math, well you know what you have to take."

"You told me you didn't have the academic smarts when we were talking a while back."

"Hey, I didn't say I was all that great. I was there for dancing instruction. Martina believed I could go places if I just applied myself."

"She really does sound like she was good for you."

"She was, Cale. That is why…" Nick choked out a cough. He took a breath. In a whisper he said, "Fuck."

"When did you get married?"

"We dated a couple years and then got married."

"How long did you, uh…" Cale realized he was now venturing towards the subject of her suicide.

"We were married four years."

"Whoa, that means you were together…six years."

"About that."

"That is a long time."

"Ya." Nick rubbed his forehead. "We had our share of downs, but it was a strong relationship."

"Why did she… I don't even know if I should ask you."

"Oh now you're going to try and not dig into my past in Las Vegas."

"Maybe I should have left the subject alone."

"Ya, well we've come this far." Nick paused. "Martina had a lot of trouble having children. She miscarried three times."

More shocking information for Cale, but he stayed silent.

"The first two were in the early years. We took a break in trying for a couple years and in our fourth year we tried again."

"I'm so sorry Nick."

"Me too. Martina was devastated by the first two miscarriages, but we got past it. Then when she got pregnant again, we were so careful."

"So she just couldn't have kids?"

"Well this is where it gets fucked. We had her younger sister come and stay with us. Jody. Pretty little girl. Fresh

195

out of high school. But she destroyed my life."

"What?"

"I don't know what was going through her head, but one night when I came home, beat, I fell asleep on the couch and she tried to give me a blowjob."

"No way."

Nick looked up to Cale's face. "Yes way. I was dead to the world, but Martina saw her sister going down on me and fainted. Unfortunately, she was on some stairs and took a hard fall."

"Unbelievable."

"Yep, it was. Imagine waking up with your pants down, your wife unconscious and a young girl screaming she's sorry."

"Nick I really don't know what to say."

"That's not the worst part. Martina lost the baby. Jody had told her I had nothing to do with what she saw, but it didn't really help." Nick remembered back to the most terrible night of his life.

Two weeks had gone since her accident on the stairs. While Nick had been at school, Martina had gotten a bottle of vodka, orange juice, her painkillers, paper and pen.

She had written a letter to Nick, while drinking vodka orange juice. She had also taken double the amount of prescribed medicine. When she had finished her letter, she had drawn a warm bath. Slicing both wrists had been easy.

Nick found her four hours later.

He had come home and the house was quiet. Martina had been mostly silent after she had been released. Nick made attempts to try and make her feel better, but no subject had gotten much of a response.

196

He wasn't surprised she was already in bed, even though it wasn't eight P.M. yet.

Entering the dark bedroom, he saw the master bathroom light was on behind the closed door. He turned on the bedroom and said loudly, "I'm home."

He took off his shirt waiting to here some noise. There was nothing.

"Hey, Martina." Throwing his shirt on the bed, he went over to the door. "Hey babe, are you alive?" Nick shouted teasingly as he tested the door and found it locked. That was strange. Neither of them locked this door.

"Martina!" Nick's voice was loud. "Please open the door or say something."

There was still no answer.

Nick kicked the door. Then he threw his body into it. The second kick did it. He saw his wife in the tub with the bloody water.

"No!" Nick screamed. He rushed to her side. His knowledge of knives knew exactly what to look for. His worst thoughts confirmed. She had slashed wrists downward. "No baby, you couldn't," he choked out. Trying to calm himself, he started thinking fast.

He raised her arms and looked for towels. Nick was crying as he shouted, "This can't be happening." He had never been this overwhelmed by emotion in his life. Quickly, he bound the wrists and then checked for a pulse on her neck. Nothing. Her eyes were open and glassy. He couldn't help himself from believing there was still a flicker of life although many signs pointed against that possibility. Nick jumped up.

"Fuck!" He screamed. A sob came heaving up like

he was puking. Nick took two deep breaths and reached into his pants pocket and pulled out his cell phone. He dialed emergency.

Explaining the situation he asked if he should drive her or wait for the ambulance. He was assured paramedics would arrive quicker than he could get her to the hospital.

Seeing her dead was like nothing he had ever experienced. Nick pulled her lifeless body out of the tub and wrapped his wife in a robe. He cradled her head in his lap and cried as he never had before in his life.

The medical team that arrived had made it fast. Nick pulled himself together when the paramedics came and he let them in.

The police came minutes later. It was a young female officer who found Martina's letter lying on a pillow of their bed.

The letter confirmed it was an obvious case of suicide by a depressed woman who had recently miscarried.

Nick felt it was much more.

To my Beloved Husband,

I love you, not only for who you are, but for what I am, when I am not with you. I love you, not only for what you have made yourself, but for what you are making me. I love you for the part of me that you bring out; I love you for passing over all my foolish and weak traits that you can't help but see. I love you for drawing out into the light my beauty that no else had looked quite far enough to find.

I forgive Jody as I hope you do. But I know our union is not healthy. You should be with a beautiful and fruitful woman. That is not me. You would never leave me, so I am leaving you. Since I know

I wouldn't be strong enough to do so breathing, this is my choice of departure. Forgive me. I love you with all my heart. You were the best thing to happen to my life. I am sorry I couldn't be the mother to your children.

I will be thinking of you as I draw my last breath.

Martina

Nick finished his story.

Cale saw Nick had tears in his eyes. He felt them welling in his own.

"Nick, I am so sorry."

"Ya, me too." Nick looked at his glass. It was almost empty. "So now you know why there is a big gap in my life I don't talk about. It's because I don't know how."

"Yeah, of course." Cale wiped his eyes.

"I'm glad I told you Cale." Nick said quietly.

"It means a lot you did. It's not lost on me that you haven't told other people about this." Cale sighed. He didn't know if he should change the subject or continue to talk about Las Vegas.

Nick looked at his friend and said, "I understand the emptiness you had when Helena died. It sucks."

"I've never understood why you were so cool to me when we first met."

"Ya, I guess it makes sense now."

"How long was it before you could smile again after Martina died?" Cale said looking at his friend.

"That's a tough one. It was a long time. I think a party some months later where I got drunk." Nick lit a cigarette. "What about you?"

"You mean when I first started to smile after Helena died?"

"Ya, do you remember?"

"Sure. I was with you at the spa. Hey, I've got an idea. Let's go out and get stinking drunk tonight and then hit a spa."

"I've created a monster."

"Yeah, a monster that can smile thanks to you." Cale grinned and jumped up. "Let's get ready."

CHAPTER 16

Apple walked into the lobby of the luxury hotel where Vesper had asked her to meet. She looked around to see if Vesper was already present. Apple had come ten minutes early. She wasn't sure why Vesper had called for this get together. It probably had something to do with Cale. He was becoming an important part of her life. She knew he was blowing off work. So was Apple. Her thoughts were interrupted by Vesper's approach.

They greeted each other in Chinese and exchanged a quick hug.

Then in English, Vesper said, "I know sometimes it is strange for Chinese people to speak in English to each other, but I would prefer it while we are here. There is less chance people will listen in."

"Vesper, English is my native language. I am more comfortable speaking English than Chinese. It's probably why I enjoy being around Cale as much as I do." Apple wasn't going to pretend she didn't know why this meeting was taking place.

Vesper smiled. "I doubt that is the only reason. He is a very good looking man."

Apple smiled back. "Yes, that's true."

"Let's get a table."

Together they walked up to the hostess stand. There was an attractive young woman to greet them. In moment they had a table in a quiet part of the restaurant.

"Do you still want to speak English?" Apple asked looking over the menu. She saw passion fruit tea on the list. It was her favorite.

"Sure. It helps me deal with Cale and Nick." Vesper gave the woman across from her an inscrutable smile.

Apple smiled back. "Good luck."

The waitress came up and took their order. Apple had hot passion fruit tea, while Vesper had hot milk tea. When the server left, both folded their napkins in their laps at the same time.

"How is work? I've been told you don't come to Escapade as much as before."

"Work is fine. I don't go out as much." Apple looked around the lounge.

"Apple, I have known you since you first moved to Taiwan and you came to my club. I know you are very smart and I like to think we are friends."

Apple watched and listened to Vesper who was dressed in a tasteful, black form fitting dress. It flattered her. Apple was quiet as Vesper spoke.

"Ever since you bought Cale and Nick together that night, I have been having trouble with both of these young men."

The waitress walked up with their tea. After the niceties were exchanged between server and customers, the waitress left. Vesper looked Apple in the eye.

"I'm not exactly sure what to do."

"I'm not sure why you are telling me this."

"Apple, Cale is a beautiful man. He has great… equipment and he knows how to use it. Very easy to get addicted to." Vesper kept her eyes on Apple's face.

"Vesper, we aren't good enough friends that I'm going to talk about Cale in bed. I know Cale has been with a lot of women, including you." Apple picked up her cup. "This is a foolish conversation. We aren't teenagers in a locker room."

Vesper picked up her tea. Sipping it slowly, she looked at Apple who was wearing a snug blue sweater dress. Her curves were apparent. It was easy to see why men found her attractive.

"Cale is a… how do you say, a… commodity." Vesper put down her cup. "Currently, my commodity."

"I think you are reaching if you think Cale belongs to anybody." Apple looked at the older woman in the eyes. "At best, you had him working for you at a time when he was searching for some sort of identity." Apple was impressed with Vesper's command of English. It was very strong.

"You think he has found his identity now? Is that why he hasn't come to work for me in almost three weeks?" Vesper was not worried about Cale leaving. She wished he would. It had been a mistake to have him become so close with Nick. Cale not coming in was a disappointment to a few women, but now Nick was taking off a lot of time also. This was a big problem.

"Vesper, I don't know exactly."

"Well he doesn't need to influence Nick."

"Oh yeah, Nick is taking off a lot of time too, isn't

he? I heard that from Shirley." Apple understood now. Shirley was a co-worker at the KTV where Apple worked and often went to Escapade to buy Nick out when she could. Apple smiled slightly.

"Yes, he is." Vesper looked down at her cup. "Apple, Nick is special. I don't know how to stop his independence. He doesn't seem to care what I think."

"Vesper, Nick is complicated. I don't know him well, but I do know that he and Cale have become very close in a very short time. It makes sense that Nick would re-evaluate his life if Cale was doing it too."

"Re-evaluate his life?" Vesper knew the word, but she feared it. "Nick has a great life."

"What was his life before you met him?"

"I don't know much." Vesper's voice was quiet. "He never talks about his past, except his brothers. Even then, it is because he is a little drunk."

"Nick likes to party."

"Do you think that's because he is hiding something?"

"Everybody hides something, Vesper."

Vesper looked from her hands to Apple. "Are you hiding something too?"

"Vesper, I'm from a rich proud Chinese family living in Ontario, Canada, yet I work in a KTV in Taiwan. I've got my secrets."

Vesper shook her head. "I hide so much of my life."

"Vesper, we have known each other at least two years. I think of you as a friend too."

Vesper looked at the younger woman. Vesper Hu didn't have many people she called friends.

"It is nice of you to say that. I run a business that would be difficult for any person, man or woman, and I feel lonely sometimes." She sighed. "Am I a bitch?"

Apple would have laughed, but saw Vesper was opening up to her.

"I don't know, Vesper. Do you hurt people on purpose?"

Vesper nodded. "Sometimes. Cale is a good example."

"What do you mean?"

Vesper sighed. "The night Cale went home with you, I had him set up with Jie so he would experience a bad night."

"I know."

"How do you know?"

"I think you can figure it out." Apple wasn't ready to implicate Nick by name.

Vesper laughed quietly. "I knew it. Nick.."

Apple smiled.

"Do you mind if I ask about the night you bought Cale and Nick together?"

Apple smiled. "Did I make them get together?"

"I don't care about that. Nick and Cale knew what was expected if you requested anything." Vesper paused, "I know you have bought many of my men and the story is always the same, you don't use them for sex."

"That is true."

"I am curious if you…"

Apple interrupted.

"Vesper, Cale and I didn't have sex the night I bought him from Jie, but there was some feeling between us. We

205

didn't have sex until I bought him with Nick."

Vesper quietly asked, "Why?"

"I wasn't ready before to be with Cale. Nick had brought us together to begin with and I… guess, I didn't want to be alone with Cale because I was scared." Apple found herself opening up.

Vesper smiled, "Having Nick there made you feel safe?"

"It sounds strange, but yes."

"You got to enjoy something I think will not happen again for any woman."

"Probably."

"How does he feel about you working at the KTV?"

"I've taken a break. I'm going to work at an import/export company. Not as much money of course, but it was time to do something else."

"I'm almost… what is the word? Jealous? No, envious. My English is getting poor."

"Your English is excellent. I really like speaking English with you. I can say what is on my mind quickly."

"Did you come to Taiwan to forget a man?" Vesper took a sip of her tea. She was comfortable asking the question.

"That's not the whole story, but it was time to get out of Toronto. I wanted to be around my grandmother."

"I made a man disappear."

"Disappear?" Apple knew what Vesper was saying.

"Very few people know this." Vesper leaned in closer over the table. She looked around casually before speak in a more hushed voice, "I loved a man who treated me wrong. He used me. I did what seemed right at the time."

"Making lovers disappear because you feel wronged is extreme."

Vesper nodded and smiled slightly. "Maybe, but I am Chinese. Honor is very important."

"Would you do that to Nick?"

Vesper tilted her head. " I am much older now. I do things differently. I could not do to Nick what I did to Jay, but I have never let Nick be in a position to hurt me like Jay did."

"His name was Jay?"

"Yes."

"I don't know. You tell me Nick doesn't mean the same as this man Jay, but every time I've seen you and Nick together, you light up."

"Light up?"

"Vesper, I don't think you are being very honest with yourself, if you say Nick doesn't mean as much to you as any man you've had in your life. You don't have a boyfriend because you have Nick."

"That is crazy."

"Is it?" Apple saw Vesper was shocked.

"I care for Nick, but what sort of woman could watch her lover be with other women and not only allow it, but encourage it?" Vesper felt queasy.

"Maybe a woman who can't admit she's in love." Apple could see she was making Vesper angry.

"You don't know me as well as you think, Apple."

"I left Canada because of a love affair gone wrong, but it wasn't the deciding factor. I left mostly because my sister and mother never listened to me." Apple coughed. "I watch people. I see a lot. My sister married the wrong man.

He beats her down with words everyday. She accepts it because she pretends it isn't happening."

Vesper stayed silent.

"My mother wanted me to be a princess. I'd tell her one thing, she would see it another way and there was no arguing with her." Apple nodded as she said quietly, "Vesper, protest all you want. Maybe you are right. But stop and think about what you would do if Nick ever left."

"It's what I'm trying to stop now. Really, Apple, Cale is a bad influence on Nick."

Apple laughed. "How is Cale a bad influence on Nick?"

"Work wise, yes. My worry is that now that Cale is finding other uh… ways to spend his time, Nick might start to think about cutting his hours."

"Vesper, why don't you spend some time with Nick the way you want to."

"I don't understand."

"Vesper, you're in love with Nick just as much as I'm in love with Cale."

Vesper blinked hard. "Is it that obvious?" She was scared of the woman's next words.

"No, not at all." Apple smiled and relaxed back into her chair.

"What about Nick? Do you think he knows? Or Cale?"

"You have those two fooled. To Nick you are a boss and Cale doesn't really factor you into his life." Apple knew what she said was true.

"Well, I guess this is our little secret."

"What can I do to help you?"

"With Nick?"

"No," Apple laughed. "Why don't I suggest Cale study Chinese? Nick would think it a good idea, but he's not going to sit in class with him."

"You think so?"

"Yes. Once, Cale was taking a shower at my place and Nick was there too. We were alone for the first time since I bought Cale and him together."

"Did you have sex with him that night when you bought him and Cale?"

"Yes. That is the point."

"I don't understand."

"Then let me finish. Nick started telling me how happy he was for Cale and me. Then I asked why he never tried to settle down. He told me he couldn't because of his past. He got all mysterious and quiet. I asked Cale later and he told me he had no idea. But I know he wasn't telling me the truth."

"Men think we are hard to understand." Vesper smiled.

"Oh no. We're just emotional on the surface. Men are emotional deep inside, where we can't reach them."

"You are a very smart young lady.

"So are you."

"I am not young. And that's why I won't ever have Nick."

"You won't win Nick's love by thinking you're not good enough for him. He's a confident man. He needs a confident woman."

Vesper smiled.

"Apple, if there is ever something I can do for you,

please just ask." Vesper Hu meant her words.

Apple smiled. "You never know when I'm going to take you up on that."

CHAPTER 17

"Come on Chris, you're always saying you want to fuck Western pussy," Nick said as he lit a cigarette for his friend. He made sure to cover the flame with his hand as a sign of respect. "She's good-looking enough, but big by Asian standards."

"Why don't you do her?"

"She's got a bit of crush on me, but who says I haven't?" Nick lit his own cigarette and gave his friend a shit-eating grin. The bar they were in was darkly lit, but Chris could see the smile.

"How do you say in English, I get second sloppy."

Nick laughed, "You mean sloppy seconds." Nick really liked Chris Wang. He was total Taiwanese in his attitude towards the world, but very open to new experiences. A perfect choice for Barb.

"I guess you and I have fucked the same woman a few times." Chris gave Nick a high-five.

Chris was one of the local guys he worked with at Escapade. More than once, women bought them out together. Often these women had Nick and Chris kiss. Asian women loved to see it for some reason. Chris handled it with aplomb every time. Like Nick, he realized it was all a part of the job and you did what the ladies wanted.

"I'd hold your hand my friend, but you know how big Western cock is compared to Asian cock. Wouldn't want you to get a complex with your first Western lady." Nick laughed knowing Chris was hung like a stallion; a strong reason for his popularity at Escapade.

"I'll pound her so hard, she won't ever think about Western dick again." Chris gave Nick a fist bump.

"I knew you were the man. Barb is fun and she has been down lately." Nick got out his wallet. They were sitting in *Up to You*, a small bar that catered to heavy drinking between the customers and employees. The employees were almost all women and the customers, men.

"Are you leaving?" Chris pulled out his wallet too.

"Nah. Just want to pay you up-front." Nick did not assume his buddy would do this for free.

"For fucking your friend?" Chris put his wallet down.

"Well, ya."

"If I asked you to fuck a friend of mine, you would charge me?"

"Nah. Of course not." Nick smiled at his friend. "But I'd expect you to pick up the tab tonight."

"Nick, you don't have to be like this."

"Ah, come on man. Let me buy our drinks tonight."

"If this woman is good, shouldn't I be buying you the drinks?"

"She is pretty good. A moaner." Nick remembered back to his time with Barbara.

"Moaner?"

"Makes a lot of noise in bed."

"Good. I'll make her have a lot of noise."

Nick picked up his glass and clicked Chris' tumbler of scotch, looking him straight in the eye. Chris returned the look instantly and both took a large swig from their drinks. They put their glasses down in unison.

"I hear Apple and Cale are going out." Chris had a low, husky voice. He was also a large-framed man. Good genetics.

Nick took a deep drag off his cigarette. "Ya, they are."

"She is a hottie."

"Ya, she is."

Chris pulled closer to Nick. "Did you get to do her when she bought the two of you?"

"What do you think?"

"Apple never did it with anyone before. I wanted to." Chris looked down at the bar. "She probably didn't do it with you either."

Nick nodded. Some things didn't need to be known even if this was guy talk. "It was all about Cale."

Chris nodded his head and grunted. He picked up his glass and did another salute. Nick immediately joined him. They both killed what was in their glasses. The whiskey tumblers went down on the bar in unison.

Chris called to the nearby bartender and ordered two more.

Nick smiled. Hanging-out with Chris was always excellent. Cale had once told him, he thought Chris was one of the coolest cats he'd ever met. The guy knew so much about everything; Nick had named him the Navigator. It had eventually evolved into Gator.

"So you and Cale are good friends?" Chris looked at the guy next to him.

"Yeah, we are." The effects of the whiskey were starting to kick-in. They were very different from beer or tequila. He was feeling happy.

"Answer me a question. Why does he do this?"

"Do what?" Nick really wasn't sure where Chris was going with the question.

"Fuck ladies for money."

Nick laughed. "Why do you do it?"

"Because I got a big dick and it should make me money."

Nick laughed. "Yeah, maybe that's Cale's reason."

Chris gave Nick a smile. "I don't know why I ask. Just sometimes he seems sad."

"You think?"

"Maybe it's different around you, but I remember once asking him about his father when I was talking about mine and he got quiet."

"His father and mother died when he was fifteen or sixteen."

Chris nodded his head silently. "Yeah, I heard that, but he never said anything."

"I think he's pretty closed about some things." Nick took a sip of his whiskey.

"Like you sometimes."

"Hey, what is this? Do you need to know something about me?" Nick knew very often when Chinese people wanted knowledge, they would talk about others to draw out an answer about the person they really wanted to know about.

214

"I think I am getting drunk and asking questions."

"Gator, you got something on your mind. Spit it out." Nick looked intently to the man next to him.

Chris smiled. He liked the name Gator. "I think I understand 'spit it out'. You want me to say what I'm thinking."

Nick nodded. "Ya."

"I think there might be trouble soon."

"What kind of trouble?"

"Uhm…, I think Vesper should be careful who gets the wiegorun cock. Sometimes just because a woman has money, she shouldn't be allowed to buy."

"Are you saying because I'm Western, I shouldn't be with some Chinese women?"

Chris picked up his glass and did a toast with Nick. "I am saying, is sometimes, the women that pay for your dick, shouldn't be with you."

"I don't get it."

Chris shook his head as he put the drink down. "That's the problem. You don't get it. Some of the women that come through Escapade, are trouble. Big trouble."

"You mean Jie."

"No Jie, is not who I talk about."

"Give me a name."

"Nick there are some women who should not buy us. Very dangerous."

"Why does Vesper let it happen?"

Chris shook his head. "I don't know. It's stupid."

"How do I be careful?"

Chris let out a deep sigh. "Maybe learn about the women you let buy you." Chris looked down at his glass.

"We have an interesting culture Nick. Taiwanese are different from Chinese and both are very different from Western." Chris paused. "They…they…How do you say, mixing?"

Nick nodded. "That sounds like it could be the word."

"Yeah, when are mixing all the rules, you better know what you are doing."

"Chris are you saying, I'm fucking up?"

"Yeah. You need to stay away from certain ladies. Vesper should say no."

"O.K., well help me out on this. Tell me who."

"I think maybe I talk to Vesper."

"You aren't going to tell me?"

"Nick it isn't the woman. It is the background she comes from. I say again, some women should not be allowed to buy us out. There are a few women we Chinese won't go with. Vesper knows this so she allows you and Cale to go instead. I say again, she is not being smart."

"Mafia babes or something like that?"

"Nick, you are not a child. You do things against the law. But if you are not very loud, people don't care. It is the same way with some of the women that come to Escapade. It is fine to drink with them, but that is it. Nothing more." Chris picked up his glass, then he continued.

"I can give you names, but maybe I'd miss somebody. Vesper should not let you be bought by some of them. I think I need to talk to her. We speak the same language."

Nick nodded. "Mr. Gator, you really are a good friend." Both did a toast and finished what was in their glasses.

"Until I do talk to her, just be careful."

Nick knew Chris' warning was to be listened to. "I'll be extra careful."

"Good. You going to call that Western woman now so I can fuck her tonight?"

CHAPTER 18

Four Days Later

"Nick, I need to see you now." The voice on the other end of the line was quiet and hoarse.

"Bad timing, Elaine. Come by Escapade and we can talk then." Nick cradled the cell phone to his ear with his shoulder as he inspected himself in the bathroom mirror.

"It can't wait that long. Whatever you want, I'll say yes." The voice was soft and inviting.

Nick moved out of the bathroom and went to his bedroom looking at his watch. It was a little after nine. He had to be at Escapade by ten thirty. "I have some free time." He thought to himself.

"I don't think I can." Nick said knowing the price was still going up. He had been with her a couple of times and she had always been more than generous. Her luxury home showed that she could afford to be liberal with her money. Nick wasn't sure, but he suspected maybe other people footed some of her bills, but she was always cool to him, so he didn't judge her.

"Nick, please come. I really need you." Now the voice was pleading. Nick felt a bit of pity for the person on the other end and smiled. "Oh what the hell, call it customer relations." Nick thought. He walked to the full-length mirror in the bedroom and inspected his face, smiling, "O.K., Elaine, but you owe me big. This really isn't a good time for me."

"Thank you."

"O.K. See you soon." He liked that her English was great. It made protracted negotiations a lot easier.

Twenty minutes later Nick was outside the nicely appointed townhouse Elaine lived in. Having been here before, he knew the garage and entrance were on the first floor. Stairs led up to the second floor where the living area opened up. It was a very roomy place with fine furniture. She was definitely a rich woman.

He rang the door buzzer. A large Chinese man opened the door.

"Uh, ni hao. Elaine zai bu zai?" (Hello. Is Elaine here?) "Who was this guy?" Nick thought to himself. He looked like a bodyguard of some sort. He was wearing all black.

"Elaine zai er lo." (Elaine is on the second floor.) The man said gruffly.

Nick stood still.

"Lai." (Come in.) The big man motioned him in. He didn't seem very friendly. Something wasn't right. The guy was big, but if he had been gunning for Nick, he could have made his move already. Besides, Nick had his blade. Just the sight of Nick's knife had turned away bigger guys than this.

Nick turned down the L-shaped hallway and stopped at the bottom of the stairs. There were four more men. All were big and all were dressed in black. This definitely didn't feel good. One of them stepped forward.

"You are Nick?" His English was heavily accented.

"Ya," Nick put up his hands in his pocket. He felt the steel in there.

"Elaine is upstairs."

"O.K." Nick didn't know what his next action should be. Every bit of experience he had told him to bolt, to get out fast. But the thugs were well positioned around him now, five men, and probably all comfortable using brute force. He saw no choice but to go on and try to play it cool, whatever was waiting for him.

"Guess the price just went up again, Elaine." Nick said to himself. He was more angry than scared. Elaine was certainly going to pay for this bullshit.

"We need to…uh…how you say, look on your body. See no gun."

"Huh?" Nick tried to act surprised. Of course they wanted to know if he had a weapon. The one who had answered the door moved closer behind him as the big one speaking to him motioned for Nick to raise his arms.

"Why?"

"Our boss upstairs. He wants to talk to you." The big man was already starting to frisk Nick's ankles.

"Do I know your boss?"

The man looked over his shoulder. He said something fast in Chinese that was unintelligible to Nick. The two by the stairs raised their jackets enough for Nick to see their holsters and the guns in them. This was not good.

"O.K." Nick raised his arms, letting the blade stay in his pocket.

The large one continued to pat him down. Nick's heart sank as the guy reached into his pocket and pulled out the knife. The blade was revealed. A slight smile passed over the man's face. He touched the blade.

"Very nice." He turned and gave it to the man who had come up from behind.

"More?" The man turned back to him and looked directly into Nick's eyes.

Nick shook his head. His anger and fear were getting harder to hide but he continued to look directly into the man's eyes.

The man stared back. "Go to bedroom." They were all staring at him. It was like being watched by well-trained guard dogs.

"Where is that?"

The man laughed revealing a huge set of dentures. He looked like a shark. "I like you. Come. Now."

Nick nodded and followed the huge man to the stairs. Two more men standing at the top looked down at him. "Well there isn't much else to do but go upstairs." He was focused now, talking himself through the situation always helped. A silent deep breath filled his lungs as he took the first few steps, following the giant up Elaine's stairs. The two at the top of the landing parted silently for them when they reached the top. The bedroom door was open. Nick followed the man in. Elaine was in a nightgown talking to an older man in a very sharp suit. They were standing.

"Keep your shit wrapped tight." Nick said to himself. "This isn't the first tough spot you've been in."

There was a brief exchange between guard and master before the older man turned to face Nick. The guard left the room.

"Ah…so this is Nick." The man's English tone and intonation were excellent. "You made good time. Thank you."

Nick looked from the man to Elaine. She was normally a very cool customer but she was obviously scared. Not a good sign.

"Yes, sir. I am Nick." Nick came forward, "May I ask who you are?"

The man extended his hand and Nick took it. The grip was hard but not overly so. Nick kept his squeeze equal.

"I am Jack." He let go of Nick's hand. "I am Elaine's benefactor."

"O.K." Nick thought, "At least the guy's English was amazing. There was a chance he could talk his way out of this."

"Elaine is quite taken with you." The man's voice got lower. He turned and slapped her, hard.

"Hey," Nick shouted, then restrained himself, by relaxing his body. Going to her aid now wouldn't be chivalrous; it would be just plain stupid.

"Elaine tells me she likes to have sex with you instead of saving herself for me." He reached to the top of her nightgown and ripped it open with a sharp downward pull exposing her breasts. Elaine's eyes, tearing but obedient, watched Jack's face as he cupped one of her white breasts. "I met her ten years ago. She is still attractive, yes, but I had her when she was still beautiful and before she turned into a slut." The man's voice was growing angry. "Go to the bed." Jack Wu pointed. She obeyed and Jack turned to face Nick.

"So, Nick, we have a problem."

222

Nick kept his eyes focused on Jack's face. "I don't understand."

Jack smiled. "You have been fucking my second wife without my permission. This makes me look bad. To be quite frank, people have died for making me look bad."

"Uhh… Jack, I didn't know she was married." Nick waited to see exactly how much Jack knew about the money exchange. The fact that Elaine was a second wife made this man very rich and above the law. In Chinese society only extremely wealthy and powerful men could marry several times. It wasn't legal, but many things in Chinese society weren't exactly legal.

"Nick, get undressed." The eyes were cold steel.

Nick pulled off his sweatshirt without hesitation or protest. He bent over and untied his shoes, kicking them off. Next he skinned off his jeans letting them fall to the floor. He stood clad in blue boxers and white socks.

"Nick, this is no time for shyness. I want everything off."

Nick's heart beat fast as he peeled off the socks and then pulled off his underwear in one fluid movement. He picked up his clothes, "Can I put them on the chair?"

The older man nodded, "Put them down and go to the bed."

"Elaine, guanle ni de mung." (Elaine close the door.)

Elaine got up from the bed and closed the bedroom door. All three were alone as Elaine came over to Jack who was standing next the king-sized bed.

Jack reached over and finished ripping off the nightgown. Nick was less then two feet away from the couple.

Jack's fingers went to Elaine's groin and started to

rub the slightly hairy mound. He got aggressive.

"You like my finger up your cunt?" Jack spat his words. His fingers worked hard and Elaine cried out.

With his other hand he grabbed her left breast and squeezed hard.

Elaine whimpered. A moment later he threw her on the bed. Jack turned to Nick.

"You have a very good body. Really excellent. What do you do to look like this?" The slanted eyes went up and down.

Nick took a deep breath. Being naked didn't bother him, or the inspection. Scrutiny was a part of his life. It was fear of not knowing the outcome that had his heart pounding in his chest. The guy was old but his movements were sure, fast and violent. It was like talking to a tiger inside the tiger's cage.

"I work out."

"A lot will be fixed here and now by you fucking Elaine with my permission. If I will it, then nothing is wrong. Do you understand my logic?"

Nick squinted, "You want to watch."

"Oh yes." Jack growled. "I want to watch."

Nick let out a deep breath.

"Come on, Nick. I know a lot about you, Friday Boy. I know this isn't against your morals."

"What do you want?" Nick asked quietly.

"I told you. Fuck her. Do it well and you might walk out of here with nothing broken." Jack smiled calmly. "Elaine, suck his dick."

Elaine moved from the bed and looked at both men questioningly. The tears had caused her make-up to run around her eyes.

"Here?" she squeaked.

"Any questions, Nick?" Jack looked hard at him.

Nick wanted to get the man's mind off his vendetta. "No sir."

Jack laughed. "Nick, I do like you." He turned suddenly and slapped Elaine again. "I told you to suck his dick. Dong ma?" (Understand?)

Elaine cried as she rubbed her cheek.

"You want us to do it on the bed?" Nick really wasn't able to read this guy. He was definitely a king shark.

"Nick, I want a show. I want to know why money has been spent on you. Stand for now." Jack yelled at Elaine, "Shenzai!" (Now!)

She leaned forward and took Nick into her mouth.

Jack backed away a little. "Good. Use that mouth you whore."

Nick allowed himself to respond. "This is just another scene." he told himself, "You've had many. Keep it cool. No big deal." He got hard quickly.

Jack used his shoe to push Elaine off of Nick. "I think you are ready for bed." Jack said blandly. He sat himself in a chair next to the bed.

As Nick got on the bed he asked, "What do you want to see, Jack?" Nick was kneeling.

"Use your imagination."

"Condom?" Nick always used one but again, he wasn't in a position to dictate much.

Jack smiled. "I like that. It means you're still worried about the future."

Nick shuddered mentally. He really didn't need to

hear those words. He looked down at Elaine who had tears slowly streaming down her cheeks. He got off the bed and faced Jack.

"Jack, I stand before you man to man. You can kill Elaine and me because you were dishonored. I can accept that as my fate. You have suffered. I will have sex with Elaine because I can see how it would make things right with you." Nick stared directly into Jack's eyes. The eyes of a great white shark, "But playing mind games isn't honorable."

Nick held his breath. Jack spoke.

"You think I'm honorable?"

"Yes." Nick spoke softly. "Men of power may have to do hard and tough things, but honor is key. You must have it." Nick knew his words were meant for a Chinese man. Giving face now could save his life.

"Nick," Jack nodded. "Have sex with Elaine and you will live."

"Jack, I want to walk-out the same way I came in. I came in good faith."

"Not to fuck Elaine?"

"Is that really the point here?

"Tell me the point again." Jack's voice was quiet. His head tilted a bit like a snake about to strike. The dark eyes added to the effect.

Nick felt his hard-on faltering a little. He twitched his groin muscles, forcing blood to his penis. This wasn't the time to look soft. "The point is you are not a man to be fucked with. Where I'm from, if you're shown respect, you show it back." They continued to look into each other's eyes while Elaine whimpered softly into her hands.

Jack stood-up slowly and gestured towards Nick.

"Get your clothes on, Nick. Please be quick." Jack's voice was quiet.

Nick moved swiftly, carefully, trying not to look scared. He pulled on his sweatshirt first.

"Nick, I am older now but I must admit that in my youth I was rash with decisions." Jack watched Nick put on his boxers.

Nick kept quiet.

"In times past you would not be leaving here."

Nick stopped dressing. It seemed like a moment to listen, to show this man he was paying close attention.

"I believe that, Jack."

Jack smiled. "I'm still tempted to have you roughed-up for fucking this bitch." He turned and spat at Elaine. "She's had everything: money, vacations, houses, anything she asked for. And she asked for a lot. She repays me by buying a man who can be had by any woman who has money. No discretion. You're a bitch." He turned back to Nick. "Finish dressing and leave."

Nick looked at Elaine. Her eyes were wide and she didn't take them off of Jack.

"Nick, I have some advice for you. Would you care to hear it?"

Nick had on his socks. His heart was beating fast. He wasn't sure Jack was really going to let him out.

"Jack, I'm sure I can only learn from it." Nick again looked Jack in his cold shark's eyes.

Jack smiled. "Nick, I think a smart, young man like you needs to get out of this city. This country. This continent. I'd do it as fast as humanly possible because it might be very uncomfortable for all of us if you didn't." A quick cough interrupted his talk. Jack cleared his throat. "I know your phone number, where you work and your address. If you're back home in your own country, there's less of a chance we might run into each other. That must not happen."

Nick nodded, "Sounds like good advice." He paused before adding, "Three days. I'm gone."

"I'd try for tomorrow."

Nick gulped slowly and obviously, "On your good advice, tomorrow it is."

Jack stepped forward as Nick put on his shoes.

"I trust this meeting will be our secret. But maybe tell your friend he should be careful and learn from your departure." Jack patted Nick's shoulder. Jack smelled like Chinese medicine and expensive cologne.

Nick nodded. Jack knew Cale worked for Vesper.

"I'll talk to him before I leave."

"He might want to consider leaving Vesper's service, too." Jack put his hands in his pockets. His eyes connected with Nick's one last time.

"I'll let him know."

"You are sure I can trust you to stay away from the authorities?"

Nick stared back, "My two brothers are in jail, along with both my parents. You don't have to worry about me going to the cops."

Jack backed away slowly, saying, "I see. In that case, there's just one more thing you can do for me…" Nick's switchblade flashed out of Jack's pocket and was buried expertly between Nick's ribs. Jack immediately let go of the weapon and it bobbed slightly as Nick took a step backwards in shock.

Nick felt himself turn pale as his right lung started to deflate.

"Take that to your grave." Then he laughed. "You see, maybe I am not so honorable."

The knife's handle protruded from his right side. It was deep and the pain was intense immediately. It was a six-inch blade but it felt like it was jammed into his spine from the front. He staggered back some more, turning to hold him-self up with the doorframe.

Outside the door he stumbled past the big guard who took him by the arm, guiding him towards the stairs. At the top of the stairs he gave Nick a soft push. Nick looked at the stairs in confusion; he was going into shock.

"Go." The guard spat under his breath.

The knife handle moved up and down as Nick took the first step, the blade was moving in his lung. He paused, wincing, trying to focus.

"Gun inya!" (Fuck you!) The guard kicked him hard between the shoulder blades, hard enough to snap Nick's head back before sending him down the stairs and into a deep ethereal blackness.

Vesper got the phone call a little after eleven in the evening. She was in Taipei and getting ready for a late dinner with her accountant.

Maria, the manager of Escapade, told her tearfully that Nick had just been taken to Rong Jung Hospital. He was in intensive care. Nick had sustained broken ribs, a concussion and a knife wound to the right lung. The only reason he was still alive was his strong body. The police intervened when Jack Wu's underlings were about to throw Nick's body in the trunk of a car. It had been a stroke of luck that two patrol cars were pulling into a small restaurant two doors down.

Jack Wu was seized in Elaine's house. Her body was found in the bathtub with multiple stab wounds. Vesper knew Jack Wu by his reputation. He was a violent man who could probably buy his way out of the situation, whether Nick lived or died.

Vesper stayed composed, listening intently and noting details. After writing down the hospital info, Vesper got off the phone. She stood a moment looking down at the table where she had put her cell phone. Vesper thought for a moment, then picked up the phone and cancelled her dinner and got herself a limo to Taichung. It would be there within a half hour.

Vesper went to her bathroom to freshen up before the three-hour journey south. She looked into the large mirror above her sink. She looked old and tired.

"Nick.", she whispered aloud. Vesper always knew she cared for the man, but until now, she hadn't known how much. Apple was right.

Vesper remembered back to their first dinner in Las Vegas.

They had been halfway through their dinner when Nick asked, "Has your life been happy, Vesper?" His voice was quiet and genuine.

She had looked into his handsome face. He had been captivating. She had known that he would be irresistible to her patrons because had been irresistible to her.

Vesper blinked back a tear as she continued to look

in the mirror.

She remembered the first time he had been bought by a customer. There had been big money offered to be the first woman. Vesper had been proud and jealous. He was no longer hers. He had never been hers.

"You made that choice," Vesper thought to herself. Or had she? Nick had been able to touch her heart, yes, but he was too wild and unpredictable. He couldn't be controlled. He had infuriated her often.

Vesper rubbed her head, then left the bathroom. There was only one person to call.

She dialed the number. The phone rang and the voice she wanted answered.

"Uncle."

Vesper was closer to him than ever since her aunt had died. But it had been decades since she'd asked for a favor like this.

"Can we speak English?" Her uncle, as of late, always wanted to have conversations in English because he planned a long trip to Vancouver and Toronto.

"Sure." Vesper swallowed. "Uncle, I need your help."

"My help?" He laughed a little. "It has been a very long time since you have said those words."

"Well, I say them now and I mean it."

"Sounds serious."

"It is very serious."

"You are making an old man nervous."

"I don't think anyone could make you nervous."

"Then you would be wrong. This phone call makes me nervous."

"Jack Wu has to pay a very huge debt for some damage done to me and my business."

"Is this the same Jack Wu that is not allowed back to Macau?"

"Yes."

"He is a man who usually can do what he wants and doesn't have to pay a price. To anyone."

"This time he has gone too far."

"Vesper he is a dangerous man. Even the police…"

"He is in their hands now."

"He must have done something very bad because he has lots of money."

"Yes, he did, but I am not sure he will be in their hands for long. You and I know, once he gets out, he will be able to leave. China, South America, Africa. His money and his connections will get him out."

"Exactly. For the same reason it will be very difficult for me to do anything."

"I will do it myself, if you cannot, Uncle." The words surprised Vesper, but she was serious.

"You always say that." Her uncle laughed a little. "It would be better if I took care of this. Not easy, but it can be done."

Vesper sighed with relief. Jack Wu was going to die. "Thank you." She paused and said, "Your English is getting quite good."

"It better. Any more of these favors and I might have to move to Canada forever." Her uncle laughed again.

"Uncle, thank you."

"You're welcome. You're my favorite niece. And you've made me a lot of money."

CHAPTER 19

Three Hours Later

Cale entered his apartment. The television was on but no one was present. He looked around the empty living room as he walked in further. Suddenly Apple appeared from around the corner. She smiled when she saw him.

"Hey," Apple said walking up and kissing him.

"How are you feeling now?" Cale looked at her face. She wasn't wearing any makeup, but she was still beautiful. Helena had never kept him enthralled the way he was with Apple.

"Better than this morning. I was really sick." Apple frowned. "When people talk about how wonderful pregnancy is and how you glow, I don't think they were factoring in freaking morning sickness."

"You're speaking very Canadian now."

"Well, that is what I am." She smiled at him again.

"I think we need to get our asses to Canada." Cale looked down to the ground. This wasn't the first time this conversation had come up.

Apple turned away and walked to their big overstuffed chair in the living room. "Cale I've told you before,

I've got to be here when the babies are born so I can be with my grandmother. The month or so after, I really have to live with her. It is tradition for a woman to go back to her family. It may be the curse of being Taiwanese, but this is something every family does. It is very important and I'd rather do it with her than my mother or sister."

Cale shook his head. He was going to suggest they get married, but the two previous times he had asked her, she told him she wanted to wait until the baby was born. Well now it was babies. They had just found a week ago there were two.

"How was school?" Apple changed the subject. She was sitting and looking at a nail that had chipped.

"O.K." Cale was studying Chinese for real now, to get his Visa. It gave him a constructive reason to stay in Taiwan, now that he had left Vesper's employ.

"Jenda ma?" (Really?)

The phone interrupted with it's loud ring.

"Stay seated, I'll get it." Cale went over to the nearby table that housed the phone.

"Way". (Hello.) Cale smiled at Apple.

"Cale, this is Vesper." Her voice sounded strained.

Cale's smile disappeared. He hadn't talked to her in over a month. It had been over six weeks since he'd left Escapade for good. Vesper had tried twice to have him come out of retirement for a party. He had refused politely both times. The last conversation had made Vesper very angry.

"Vesper, how are you?" Cale asked politely.

"Not very well." Vesper choked. She felt herself ready to cry as she talked to Cale.

"What is wrong?" Cale thought she was going to

plead with him to work one more time.

"Nick is in the hospital. ICU. It doesn't look good." Vesper lowered her voice. "They think he is going to die. If he wasn't so fit he would be dead now."

"What happened?" Cale was stunned. He had talked to Nick earlier this evening.

"Nick was stabbed by a very bad man." Vesper's voice got quiet. "Elaine Phat's boyfriend." Vesper whispered, "It's my fault."

"This can't be happening!" Cale felt a lump begin to rise in his throat. "Where is he?" Cale's voice was filling with panic.

Apple got up from her chair. She could tell something was wrong.

"Rong Jung hospital." Vesper's voice stayed low.

"Do you know Rong Jung Hospital?" Cale asked Apple, now standing next to him. Her face wore an expression of worry. She nodded.

"Vesper, I'm going there now. Anything we can do for you?"

"I don't want him to die, Cale." A sob escaped. She pulled herself together. "I'll see you soon. I'm still taking care of some things." She was getting the names of everyone involved in the stabbing. Vesper was determined all would wish they had never breathed air on this planet.

"Take care of yourself." Cale said quietly.

"You too."

The line went dead.

"What happened?" Apple asked anxiously.

"Nick's been stabbed." Cale said shaking his head in disbelief.

"Is it bad?" Apple took a deep breath.

"Very bad, I think." Cale let out a deep sigh. "Unbelievable."

"Why?"

"I know it has something to do with a customer's boyfriend, but that is about all Vesper told me."

Apple shook her head.

Cale started to get angry. "Fucking assholes." He wanted to hit something.

"Let's get over to Rong Jung."

"Yeah, let's go." Cale's mind was spinning.

"Let's take a taxi." Apple said getting a light green jacket that was on a coat rack by the door.

Forty minutes later found them in Rong Jung Veteran's Hospital. Although modern, the corridors were filled with patients; most were elderly, lying on metal stretchers, waiting.

To Cale, the smell was a place of sickness. Body odors from the aged people, medicine mixed in the air and began to make Cale feel noxious. Flashes of his time in Bali came and left.

Apple went looking for information, leaving Cale to himself in a hallway near the front lobby. His mind was now thinking of Nick and a time they were at a sauna. It had been the day after, Apple had bought him and Nick for the night.

Both were in a small pool with warm swirling water. The sauna was deserted except for a few attendants.

"You've been quiet today. You O.K.?" The water was waist high. Nick splashed around a little with his hands.

"Fine." In truth, Cale was a little freaked out with his friend.

"I don't think you are." Nick looked at his hands. "Especially with me."

Cale looked over at Nick. "If I wasn't O.K., I wouldn't be here now." His voice was slightly defensive.

"Hey, relax. It was like pulling teeth to get you to come." Nick came closer to where Cale was standing. "Are you O.K. about last night?"

"Last night was weird for me. What do you want me to say?" Cale didn't want to talk about the night before. Too much strangeness went on for his upbringing. "Give me some space on this one."

"Dude, I'm not giving you any space because you might end up scared of me. I can't let that happen. I'm not gonna stand on the sidelines and pretend I don't see what I see." Nick's voice had gotten louder; then he quieted down. "That's not me Cale; you know it." Nick looked into Cale's eyes.

"I'm not scared of you." Cale words sounded hollow.

"It's what you say, but your eyes and actions say something else." Nick moved away and splashed the water again.

Cale stayed silent but let out a sigh.

Nick looked up and smiled, "Apple had a good time."

Cale also broke a slight smile. "Yeah, I think she did."

"Bet she doesn't buy me out anymore, goddamn it." Nick kept his tone light.

Cale remembered the passion that Apple and he had. Nick had gone and taken a shower when their real lovemaking started. But Nick had seen enough.

"Nick, I really don't want to talk about last night." Cale turned away.

"Why?" Nick looked up from the water.

"There are a lot of reasons, man." Cale turned back to face Nick. "Just drop it."

"Nope." Nick stood still. "Give the most important reason you don't want to talk about last night and then I'll drop it."

"That makes a lot of sense. Then you're going to want to talk about it and I don't want to." Cale was looking at the steps leading out of the pool.

"Face me, Cale." Nick's voice was deep. "Face me. Don't run."

"I didn't really like we had sex with Apple together." Cale said slowly.

"Well, she paid for it." Nick scratched his nose. "For the record, I think she's smitten with just you. Lucky dog."

"Can we stop?" Cale didn't like the conversation at all.

"No. Fuck no." Nick moved closer. "You are not facing me about this." Nick gave a little cough.

"You know what, I'm getting a little tired of all the overwhelming attention you are giving me. Let it drop. I'm serious."

"The street guy inside me, says no fucking way." Nick was now within a foot of Cale.

"Do you have to get so close Nick? I really don't like it." Cale was remembering last night."

Nick didn't move. "I was pretty close to you last night. No clothes then either." He folded his arms.

"Last night I was being paid to be close to you; now

I have a choice." Cale looked straight into Nick's eyes.

Nick got angry, "Blow me." He dropped his arms.

"Think you're the guy in this pool with all the knowledge in that department." Cale's voice was low.

"It's a good thing I love you bro, or I would kick your ass or die trying." Nick's voice was a growl. He pushed back his wet hair. "You can keep on saying stupid shit to me or you can be the friend I know you are and tell me what is wrong."

"Nick, I am a bit freaked out about that moment when you grabbed me and hugged me, telling me how much you 'fuckin' loved me." Cale looked down into the water.

Nick stared at Cale who had his head still down. "I make no apology for being happy for you as I saw Apple repairing damaged goods. I really think you're over Bali now. Or well on the way to being over it. That is what that hug was. Being happy for you. I don't get the problem."

"You really don't get that a hug in bed is a little too much for the average guy?" Cale looked up.

"Cale, redneck you may be, but face this hard reality, we are not average guys." Nick let out a little laugh. "Dude we had sex in front of each other hardcore. While I was getting a blowjob, fucking or making out with her, you were fucking, getting a blowjob or making out with her. And we were getting paid. Don't give me this average guy shit."

"The hug weirded me out." Cale was now trying to explain.

Nick backed away a little. "Sorry to hear that." Nick gave a small cough. "I guess I've figured that out now. Guess I know why too."

"Yeah, because two naked guys shouldn't be hugging each other in bed where sex has been going on." Cale finally got it out. Nick was wrong on this one.

"Could it also be because of my past when I hustled to stay alive?" Nick looked down at the water again.

Cale admitted to himself, Nick was right. "It probably has a little to do with it."

"Cale I thought we were beyond this. I kept our physical contact to a minimum so you could be comfortable in bed and enjoy Apple." Nick still didn't look up. "I was just really happy for you."

The words touched Cale. He had wronged his friend.

"Nick you're right." Cale's voice was low. "I've been really stupid."

"I know you have." Nick looked up. "It's why I had to bring you to the fuckin' spa."

"I'm not sure I get that." Cale stayed put looking at his friend.

"If I didn't have us stripped down, this talk was probably going to go nowhere." Nick splashed a little water at Cale.

Cale looked Nick straight in the eye. "I get I misread last night, but we could have talked about this somewhere else."

"Don't think so. We started this friendship in a place like this. Good place to save it."

"You really think I'd throw our friendship away because of last night?"

"Ya, Cale I do. You doubted my intentions. What comes next? I'd say that's damage done, if I don't call you on it."

"That was well said." Cale stared at his friend, the water making gurgling sounds in the background.

"I have my good days." Nick looked down at his hands in the water.

"Nick come here."

"Why?" Nick looked up.

"I want to give you a hug."

Cale's thoughts were interrupted by Apple.

"Cale, Nick is on a respirator." She sighed. "Right now they are worried about infection. They had to sew-up some of his lung."

Cale shut his eyes. "Jesus."

"The doctor I talked with said, if Nick doesn't get an infection, he could pull through."

"I guess it is good news."

"It's hard to say Cale. But we can't look in on him right now. We can tomorrow at nine in the morning." She said lowly, "We could wait here in the lobby, if you want."

Cale looked at Apple. "Think I have to spend the night here, babe." He held back the tears that were welling up. "I can't take the chance of not being here if something goes bad." Cale sighed.

Apple nodded. She smiled. "I'll stay."

"You don't have to." Cale got closer and reached for her hands. They were soft and warm.

"Yes I do." She squeezed his hands gently.

He smiled at her. "I'm glad you are staying."

"Are you hungry?" Apple had seen a dumpling shop on the street when they entered the hospital.

"A little," Cale said, noticing suddenly that he was famished.

"I saw a place downstairs where I can get something to eat." She didn't ask him to come.

"I'll go with you, but I want to get back here as quick as I can."

Cale held her hand as they walked down the bustling corridor.

CHAPTER 20

One Week Later

The nurse with the nice smile waved Cale on to the first door past the reception desk. She had just called a taxi for Apple to go home so she could get ready for work. They had looked in on Nick to see him sleeping earlier. Cale was staying until Nick awoke. He pushed open the doublewide door.

Inside Nick's private room the lights were off. The windows provided a panoramic view of the city that reflected enough light to give the large room a daytime feel. He saw Nick was awake.

"Hey, Mac the Knife? Mac in here?"

Nick was lying stiff in bed, propped up with tubes in his right arm.

"Yo." Nick said, shifting a bit. The T.V. was on. It's reticulated arm extended over his bed table breakfast. "Come on in." He smiled.

"Apple and I were here earlier but you were sleeping. Then the nurse just told me you woke up." Cale moved close to the bed and they slapped hands.

"The hot one at the desk?" Nick smiled and stifled a cough. His smile ended in a sudden grimace of pain.

"Apple, will come back later." Cale looked over Nick lying in bed. "So this guy thought he could just stab Nick Young and get away with it?" Cale feigned a punch at Nick's jaw.

Nick moved quickly to guard, but not as fast as usual, "He did get away with stabbing me." Nick pushed aside his dinner table and Cale with it, forcing him backwards as he laughed. "Got you beat from the bed, got you beat from the bed!" He laughed out loud despite the intense pain. "Fucker! Hurts! Jesus."

"One of these days you're gonna laugh yourself to death." Cale reached for Nick's glass of water.

"No, no. I'm O.K." He felt his side and grimaced again, "It's not my throat, it's my ribs. Plus I'm finally done coughing up all that shit from my lungs. A lot of black shit."

"You could probably get high of that stuff."

"Probably. But coughing is hell. It hurts so much. Doesn't feel like a stab wound as much as it feels like I got shot."

"Did you get shot before?" Cale was only half serious.

"No. Stabbed is bad enough. I mean it feels like, all the way through." Nick smiled mischievously. "Things could be worse. Nursie told me, a lot of the ladies have been dropping by to check in on me."

"Came to check on their equipment, eh?" Cale made as if to lift up Nick's bed sheets, causing Nick to stir. He winced in what looked like severe pain.

Cale looked at the tubes still protruding from his friend's chest. There was a stack of monitors next to the bed.

"They shut that thing off just before you came in," Nick said, pointing to one of the devices, "I guess I stopped leaking."

"It's much better if you don't leak." Cale sized him up. Nick's voice was weak and seeing him helpless like this was disheartening. His eyes seemed sunken and he had never looked so pale.

"Supposedly you're prone to leak after you get stabbed and thrown down stairs. It's O.K., they have all the proper equipment. But now, I stopped leaking and it's a lot easier to breathe." Nick took a cautious breath, "See?"

"Good for you. You can breath without leaking." They both smiled.

"I'm going to ask you a favor now." Nick took on a grave expression, made more severe by his sunken features. He pushed the TV away. "Can you get me a jug of orange juice and some ice?"

"Sure." Cale moved as if to leave.

"Wait…" Nick said, raising his arm. Cale stopped and turned to him. "Big orange juice, lots of ice." Nick stared at him.

"Got it." He stared at Nick, waiting for more requests, but Nick only waved him off with a humorous, "Ta ta."

Cale left through the large door and passed the reception desk on his way to the elevators. The nurse beamed at him from behind the desk and Cale smiled back.

The elevator took him down to the lobby fifteen floors below. Cale could see the familiar colors of 7-11 as soon as the doors opened. Heading straight to the back of the store, he picked up a large jug of orange juice and a bag of ice.

On the way back up to Nick's room the elevator was crowded with people. An old woman in the corner was coughing loudly, her adult son trying his best to console her. The rest of the people in the elevator looked at the ground, Cale included. He hated hospitals.

Everyone seemed to be getting off on different floors. They stopped at every other floor and ten minutes later, he got off on fifteen.

As soon as the doors of the elevator opened Cale sensed something was wrong. The nurse was gone, the telephone left askew on her desk. A binder lay open on the floor. Cale bolted for Nick's room.

Inside there was a ball of kinetic energy over Nick's bed. A male nurse wearing an operating mask was wrestling with Nick, while the nurse screamed and hit his back with her bare fists. The man was very skinny, medium height, and faced Nick to damage his injured friend as they grappled. The man's wild eyes remained on the nurse. He had obviously not counted on her involvement.

"Hey!" Cale launched a running drop kick on the stranger, just missing the nurse, who was apparently so startled by this latest combatant that she fell straight backwards and hit her head on the tile floor. The stranger crashed into the stacks of equipment next to Nick's bed, tangling himself in the wires as he toppled with the machine.

"Ah!" Nick cried out as a tube ripped out of his chest. He glanced down and yanked out the remaining IV tubes taped to his hand. When Nick looked up, the man had disappeared, but Cale was kicking something.

The nurse stood up, holding her head, and then ran

out of the room. Cale continued to kick.

"Mother fucker!" Cale stopped kicking.

Nick looked down at the mess of equipment and saw the stranger, sprawled, broken and bloody between his bed and the toppled monitors.

"That fucker had a syringe. Where's the syringe?" Nick sounded surprisingly calm to Cale, "You just don't let a guy like that inject shit into your IV. Look at his shoes."

Cale was breathing heavy. The repeated kicking had been more of a reflex response than anything else. As he regained his composure, the attire of the male nurse became more distinct. Besides his green hospital coat and poorly fitting scrubs, the man lying unconscious on the floor was no more a nurse than Cale or Nick. One of his dirty flip-flops had come off in the scuffle and the leg of his scrub pants had been pushed up exposing a tattoo. The kind of tattoo that spoke of the underworld.

"Probably desperate to impress someone. Probably by himself, but we should really take off." Nick started to get out of the bed, wincing as he did so.

"No way. No way. That nurse went to call the cops. Chill out." Cale grabbed him by the shoulders, "You don't have to stay in here but don't take off," He smiled a funny, adrenaline charged smile, "You might start leaking again." They shared a quick fraternal laugh that ended in a wince for Nick. They looked down one more time at the failed assassin.

"Fucker's probably a drug addict. He's sure no professional." Nick spat onto the shoe of the unconscious killer. "Guy tried to inject some shit into my tube. Right in front of me. He's shaking the whole time and telling me in Chinese he's a doctor. Then the nurse comes in…" Nick erupted into a quick burst of laughter. "She starts yelling and hitting him right away. He tries to inject anyway and then I'm like, what the fuck?"

"Then what happened?" Cale watched a slow runnel of blood make it's way outwards from the unconscious man's head.

"Then you came in. Thanks buddy, who knows what would have happened if it had just been that nurse and the gimp here."

The nurse returned, leading the way for a frightened policeman. The cop was sweating and seemed to be the most nervous person in the room. He spoke quickly in Chinese with the nurse while everyone looked down at the fallen man. After some dialogue that Nick contributed to as well, Cale watched the policeman bend down and handcuff the unconscious suspect to Nick's hospital bed.

That night, after some cursory interviews with the police, and a few phone calls to Vesper, Nick was moved to a different hospital by stretch limousine.

"'Just for safety', she says." Nick smiled at Cale who was helping him out of the limo into a wheelchair at Jun Shin Hospital, "That's what she said." Nick held his side as they moved across the expansive square leading towards the front doors of the hospital. It was late and the front of the place was poorly lit.

"What do you mean?" Cale looked down at his charge.

"She's pissed. I hope she doesn't try to mess with this situation much more."

"Jack's the guy who tried to put Drain-O in your IV?

I thought the cops have him."

"The cops have Jack but he isn't the man who tried to kill me in the hospital. That guy was some speed freak who probably just wanted to impress the big boss. He overheard something or his brother is a bodyguard, could have been a lot of things. The guy was a punk. I was lucky." Nick stopped and turned into the wind to face Cale. "Jack Wu is who stabbed me and killed his girlfriend. If Jack had really ordered me dead, my guess is I'd be dead." Nick laughed a little, before stopping to catch is breath. "Then again, I think he wanted me dead last time around." Nick shook his head as he continued speaking. "I get the impression Vesper is way more connected than I realized."

"Vesper has a strong personality and I for one, wouldn't want to fuck with her." Cale said having spoken with her earlier. Vesper had been brief and explicit with her orders.

"Meet Nick right away and don't attract attention. I want him out of the hospital without a lot of people watching. The doctors and nurses have already been paid to help and keep quiet."

It had been the first time Vesper had warned him to be clandestine. When he had left her that morning she had seemed more like a general at wartime than a threatened business owner.

"I think you're right. God knows how many times I've been flirting with danger, pissing her off."

"So speed freak back at the Rong Jung Hospital is going to jail?"

"Ya. Ya. He fucked with me and he fucked with a nurse. Dude's going to the big house. He probably just got out last week."

"Why the hell would a person, gangster or otherwise, just take it upon themselves to kill a man?"

"Drug or gambling problem. Mr. Tough Guy back there couldn't even handle a nurse and a stabbing victim. He was more scared than we were. Probably just trying to earn some quick respect. That's the way the gangsters work here sometimes. If you can solve a big boss's problem without being asked, you get props."

Cale opened the doors and pushed Nick into the main lobby.

"What's in here?" Cale said, aware of the weight from carrying Nick's overstuffed backpack.

"Everything I need."

After being registered Nick found his new room considerably more luxurious than his former one. Cale carried in Nick's belongings and set them down on the bed.

Nick opened the suitcase still sitting in the wheelchair, "We still have the orange juice, but I think we'll need fresh ice." Nick removed the bottle of orange juice and then started to pull himself up on the bed.

Cale came immediately to his side and helped his friend get in bed.

"They probably have ice in the cafeteria. Why do we need ice again?"

"For this," Nick said, pulling a bottle of Hendrick's gin out of a large pocket on the side of the backpack. "Barb was one of the ladies that stopped by earlier. She dropped this off. We get the orange juice action, we're golden."

"Barb came by."

"Yeah, with Chris."

"Chris? Oh, Gator."

"The same." Nick was grateful the IV's were done as he lay in bed. He was still weak, but he could move around by himself. The wheelchair was for long distance.

"Together?"

"It looked that way."

"I had no idea they hung out."

Nick propped himself up on the pillows as Cale started to unpack Nick's belongings.

"Call me Cupid. The night before fun with Jack and my knife, I asked Chris to hook up with Barb. Anyway, both of them told me gin was medicine first before anything. Invented by the Dutch. I bet you didn't know the Dutch were the first Europeans to settle Taiwan?"

"You are right, I didn't. That is pretty wild." Cale put the six books Nick had on the stand next to the bed.

"What is really wild is Gator warned me about something bad like this."

"Getting stabbed?" Cale couldn't help asking the next question. "Do you think he knew it was going to happen?"

"I asked him today. He wasn't surprised when he heard about me being stabbed by a jealous boyfriend, but he didn't know Jack Wu."

"Glad I'm done with that world."

"Yeah, maybe me too. Gator said I should be very careful now."

Cale sat on the bed careful of Nick's legs. "What are you going to do?"

"I don't know. I feel pretty fucked up right now." Nick let out a deep sigh.

"You want my advice?"

Nick kept his voice quiet, "I'm not sure." Then he laughed a little. "Who else would I listen to, Cale?"

"I think you need to go back to school. Get stateside. You need to get out of Taiwan. I don't want you to go, but I'm worried. Who knows how many other chicks have rogue boyfriends? Or how many other speed freaks want to kiss Jack Wu's ass by killing you?"

"Yeah, I think that is what Gator was saying. Barb also said her connections to the mafia mentioned I was in trouble. Makes me feel very popular right now."

"Fuck." Cale let out a deep sigh of his own.

"Sounds like we need some ice to get those drinks going." Nick slapped Cale playfully on the back.

"O.K., doc." Cale smiled as he got up and left the room.

CHAPTER 21

One Day Later

"You look good for a man who has cheated death twice." Vesper smiled as she walked into the new room.

"It is the new hospital accommodations. Anything is better than that shit hole I was in before." Nick felt warm seeing Vesper walk in the room.

"You wouldn't listen to me before when I tried to move you here days ago." Vesper walked up to the bed. This was a private clinic for the very rich. There weren't many in Taiwan of this caliber.

"Vesper's right again." Nick was comforted to see her.

"Believe it or not Nick, I don't always try and be right concerning you."

"Whoa. That is sort of mysterious." Nick was relaxed in his position. "Have a seat on the bed."

Vesper looked him up and down. He seemed much better than the first time she had seen him in a hospital bed. She sat down on the bed next to him.

"Nick, I think we need to have a talk about your future."

Nick saw Vesper was nervous. He stayed silent watching her closely.

"It might be time for you to think about leaving Taiwan."

Nick stayed silent.

"Of course I don't want you to go. But there is quite a lot I can't control although I like to think I can."

"Vesper, I know you control more than you let on."

"I'm not so sure about that."

"What are you trying to say here? I'm still in danger?" Nick looked into her eyes. "I know that. Working for you has always been dangerous."

Vesper nodded. "I think you are right."

"I'm a big boy Vesper. I know I'm only still alive because of you. Cale played interference, no doubt, but my security has been in your hands and I know it."

"It's safe here, for now."

"I am a lot of trouble to you aren't I?"

"You are just starting to realize that now?" Vesper gave his arm a little tap. She felt happy to be sitting next to him.

"Come on, I'm not all that bad." Nick sat up.

"Bad or good, I think it is time you got out of here. There is always going to be some crazy person out to kill you because Jack did them a favor."

"Where is he?"

"Remarkably, he is in jail. Even he can't murder a girlfriend and not pay the price. The police in Taiwan are getting more modern. You can't just buy off the judges anymore." Vesper lowered her voice as she thought out loud, "Having the media jump on this didn't help. Killing her and almost you, has brought more attention than he bargained for."

"No media has visited me."

"Partly the police, partly me. This really has gotten very messy."

"You're telling me. God, I wish I had never answered the phone that day, much less gone over there."

"Nick you are alive. Jack was going to hurt you no matter what, so maybe it worked out for the best. He will be paying the price for this sooner or later in jail."

"If this was the best…"

"I think you know it could have been much worse. He could have cut off your instrument."

Nick laughed. "My instrument? That's cute Vesper." Nick pulled down his sweat pants to reveal his penis. "This guy probably isn't going to be up for action anytime soon."

Vesper took the flaccid organ in her hand. She stroked it up and down. She found it beautiful to look at. It began to thicken.

"What are you doing Vesper?" Nick had only pulled his pants down as a joke.

"Do you want me to stop?" Vesper said still stroking.

"Someone could walk in."

"Neither one of us are shy about something like this." She tightened her grip. Nick's body was reacting.

"Aw fuck…" Nick slid down his pants a bit.

"I think you are responding well." It was true. He was fully erect in her hand.

She leaned down and kissed the tip, using her tongue to lick the head.

"Jesus." Nick had not expected this when Vesper had entered the room.

Vesper grasped harder. She had Nick in her power. He wasn't going to push her away.

"Vesper…" Nick let out a moan. It had been weeks since he had given up any sperm.

"Relax Nick," she said and then kissed his lower belly.

Nick settled back and let the inevitable climax occur. It was an explosion.

Vesper stayed quiet as she milked the last of his ejaculation.

"Whoa, that was quite a load I had built up."

"I know. I figured it was time for you if some nurse hadn't done it already."

"Nurses don't seem concerned about that. They have all been very professional, unfortunately." He watched as Vesper got some nearby tissue and cleaned.

"You should be happy I came by." She pulled his pants up.

"I'm always happy to see you." Nick was feeling drained, but content.

"Back to the matter at hand. The doctor wants you here for one more week and then therapy."

"How long for therapy?"

"I don't know. I asked if you could do a plane ride. He said yes if you have a row to yourself." Vesper got up and threw the tissue in a nearby trashcan.

"You really are serious about me getting out of here soon."

"Nick, I told you before, I don't want you to go." Vesper said coming back to the bed. "But I don't think I could face seeing you in a hospital again."

Her last words were quiet.

Nick was touched.

"Things can happen in the U.S. too. Leaving Taiwan doesn't ensure my safety."

"Yes it does. Besides, I'm shutting down my clubs. It's time for me to get out."

"Are you kidding me?" Nick was incredulous.

"I've made my money, Nick. I'm rich and it is time to quit."

"What are you going to do?" He couldn't believe she was quitting her business.

"I don't know."

"This seems to be a very rash decision."

"No. I've talked about it with the right people and there is strong agreement for me to get out. Jack Wu and friends won't be able to attack what is no more. Also, the police are not going to look the other way much longer."

"All because of me." Nick's voice was low and sad.

"No, Nick. It could have been many other things or one of the other boys. You are not the only one gangster girlfriends use for recreation. I should be happy it didn't happen before. Also, I'm not young any more. Nick, I can't recruit like I used to."

"That's bullshit and you know it." Nick sat up with a slight jab of pain going to his side. He grimaced.

"Be careful," Vesper admonished him.

"Cale thinks I should go back to school and get a degree. Why don't you come to America with me?" Nick said quickly.

Vesper smiled. She loved hearing the words. "Tempting, Nick. You are going to need someone to look after you, but I think it is going to take a little time to settle my affairs here. You go first and maybe I'll visit."

"I'm only saying yes, if you come and see me."

"Nick," Vesper said sweetly, "It almost sounds like you care."

Nick smiled. "Don't let it go to your head."

A nurse walked in and greeted them.

CHAPTER 22

Six Months Later

Cale was sitting on the sofa waiting for Apple to get out of the bathroom. In his hand was a lesson for tomorrow, but he couldn't focus. Today was the day. Apple and he would be parents very soon. The doctors were giving her a C-section.

The phone rang. Cale answered. It was Apple's grandmother. She spoke Chinese asking for Apple.

Cale still struggled with the language. He told her they were leaving by cab in a matter of minutes.

Getting off the phone, Cale went to the bedroom. He walked over to a chest of drawers and opened the top one. Inside was a walnut box that held his jewelry. Getting the box out, he opened it up and pulled out the locket that had not been worn since he'd put it on Helena. Today was the day to give it to Apple. He opened the heart and saw the picture Helena had of him. Cale wasn't sure if he should pull it out or not. He decided it would be best for a new one. There was actually room for two, so maybe they could put the twins pictures in it. Whatever she wanted. He felt it was time for her to have it. Cale put it in his pocket and walked to the bathroom. He knocked on the door.

"You O.K.?" The doctor had given her iron pills in her seventh month of pregnancy because her blood levels showed her to be a little anemic. Apple worried that the children might be affected and sometimes went into depression. She had been in one earlier this morning.

"I'll be out in a minute. Washing my face now." Apple called to him through the door.

"I'm calling the taxi." Cale walked away. He was nervous. At least he had gotten Apple to marry him. Although he was Catholic, Cale wasn't worried about having a religious ceremony. Apple had been talking about moving to Canada.

After speaking to the taxi, he sat back down on the sofa. When they got to Canada, Cale wanted to finish school. It was time to pick his life back up and having a family intensified his determination. Nick had left three months ago and had taken up the challenge to get back into school. All signs pointed to leaving Taiwan. He was very happy Apple wanted to go to Canada.

Cale sat a few more minutes in silence waiting for Apple. He wondered what it was going to be like to meet her parents. Her grandmother was friendly, but the communication barrier was immense, so he didn't feel close to her the way Apple was. He knew she was the reason he couldn't get his family over to Canada quicker.

Cale smiled to himself. He was grateful Apple was his partner. She was a great wife.

His cell phone rang. It was the taxi. Cale spoke Chinese to the best of his ability, telling the driver they would be down in five minutes.

"Where was she?" he thought to himself. He went by

the bathroom and saw the door was shut. He tried it. The door opened but something was preventing him from getting inside. Immediately he knew it was Apple.

"Apple, Apple," he kept repeating. With her body blocking the doorway, Cale wasn't sure how to get in. He couldn't shove her aside. "Apple, baby, get up!"

There was no movement.

"O.K., stay calm," he told himself. He went to his cell phone and called Apple's doctor.

Cale was relieved to hear Dr. Chen's voice. He explained what was happening. The doctor told him an ambulance would be sent. In the meantime, Cale had to get the bathroom door open.

The cell called again. It was the taxi. Cale asked the man to come up to his apartment. Two of them would be more effective.

The driver was up in minutes. In his pocket, he had a Swiss army blade. He went to the top of the door and worked on the hinges.

"Good idea," Cale said in English.

Within minutes they were in the bathroom. Apple was still unconscious. Cale heard the ambulance come to the building. The taxi driver was saying unintelligible words to him. Cale didn't pay any attention. He put a cool rag on top of her forehead. Her skin was pale white. Right now she looked grey.

The knock on the front door got him up. It was the paramedics. They had an oxygen tank along with a stretcher.

It didn't take them long to get Apple out the door. Cale paid the taxi driver and thanked him. Then he grabbed his coat and ran to catch the ambulance. They were finished putting her inside when Cale got to the vehicle. The drivers went to the front seat, and a paramedic made room for Cale to sit.

Cale explained he was Apple's husband.

The paramedic nodded. Then he went back to examining Apple.

Cale was at a loss. He had no idea why Apple would faint. Was she scared of the operation? His mind was starting to jumble. He was remembering back when his parents died. Cale stopped himself. This wasn't the same. Apple wasn't going to die. He looked at the woman he loved under the oxygen mask. She had been a little grumpy when they had gotten up, but that was the only sign he could think of that she was out of sorts.

"If something happens…" Cale stopped himself again. "Don't do this. She has just passed out because she is carrying twins full term." He wished Nick were still in Taiwan.

The siren wailing didn't help, but he was grateful. Traffic in the city was terrible, but the ambulance was still moving with speed.

"Could the day get any worse?" he asked himself. Six hours later, he found it could.

The impossible was happening. The doctor explained it well in English. Her anemia brought major complications to the operating table. When she hemorrhaged during the birth there was no way to stop the bleeding. The babies lived, but the mother was going to die. He couldn't believe it, especially after she regained a drowsy, lethargic kind of consciousness. They gave her a strong painkiller but she was still awake and able to speak with Cale.

Cale yelled himself hoarse in the hallway, arguing with the doctor to do more for her. In the end he was told she should not even have lived through the birth.

He was ushered into the room which Apple shared with another woman convalescing. Apple's grandmother was kneeling by the bed, crying loudly.

Apple spoke softly in Chinese and the old woman got up. Cale was looking at all the monitors hooked-up to his wife.

Cale went to her bedside.

"The babies are beautiful." Cale's voice was quiet.

"I saw them, but I'm so weak. I couldn't hold them."

"Plenty of time later."

"Am I dying Cale? My grandmother, the nurses, doctors, all are acting strange." Apple shut her eyes. "I'm so tired and like my body is floating around. It's weird."

Cale took a deep breath.

"Baby, you aren't dying. You had a really hard birth. There was a lot of blood and that has made you weak. But you aren't out of my life anytime soon."

Apple smiled. "I needed to hear that. Any other person but you, I probably wouldn't believe them." Eyes still shut, she said her last words, "God, I'm glad you always have to tell the truth."

Cale stayed with her until the end an hour later.

After checking on the babies one last time, he felt it necessary to get out of the hospital. On the way out, he saw a woman that resembled Helena. Cale held back a shout and ran outside quickly.

Cale found himself walking to a small park. It was

empty although the early morning hospital traffic was bustling. He saw a bench and sat down. Cale covered his face with both hands. His parents' deaths had blown him away. Helena, Gary and Tina had been a horrible ordeal.

He started to cry hard, letting the tears fall freely. He sobbed into his hands and cried, "I don't believe this."

The tears came fast. He really was at a loss. It seemed impossible that Apple was gone, and so quickly, but he'd watched it happen. There was no mistaking that she was gone forever.

Again he found himself wanting to talk to Nick. It would be two in the afternoon overseas. Chances were Nick would be around if he wasn't in a class. Cale pulled out his cell phone. Nick's number in New Jersey was already entered.

The phone rang. Cale took three deep breaths. The ringing continued. Then Nick's message came on telling the caller to leave a number.

"Nick, this is Cale. There were some complications with the birth of the twins. Apple died." Cale's voice cracked. "I could use your voice right now, bro. Give a call no matter when." He got the last words out with a considerable effort and burst into tears. Taking a deep breath he got control again. Cale clicked off the phone after seeing it was a little after two in the morning. He wasn't ready to go home yet. Escapade came to mind, but that was almost as bad as going home. Everyone would sympathize with him and try to make him feel better. He didn't want to buried in sympathy. He wanted Apple back.

"You are not an easy person to find." The voice was gentle, coming from behind. It was Vesper. Cale turned around to face her, wiping his tears.

"Do you mind me joining you?" Vesper was dressed in a black, stylish dress with matching jacket. The voice stayed soft.

Cale nodded and moved over. There was a moment of silence.

"I guess you know about Apple," Cale said barely above a whisper. He choked on the last word.

"Yes, Cale, I know." Her voice stayed gentle, but there was trembling in the tone.

"Vesper…" He let out a deep breath. "I'm out of my depth here. I have two babies and…" Cale couldn't finish his thoughts. A sob came instead.

Vesper stayed silent. She put her arm around his shoulder.

Cale started to cry.

"Vesper, I lied to her. I told her she was going to live and I knew she wasn't." Cale couldn't stop crying, "I never lie and I lied to her." The tears kept coming. He didn't care about holding back. He had never lost control like this in his life.

Suddenly his phone rang. Cale's heart jumped. It had to be Nick. Looking at his phone, he saw he was right.

"Can you answer it?" Cale handed the phone to Vesper. He wiped away his tears as he took some deep breaths.

Vesper took the phone.

"Hello," Vesper said in English.

"Vesper?" Nick's voice was surprised. "I thought I had Cale's number."

"You do."

"He called me about Apple. What happened?"

Vesper got up from Cale. She kept her voice quiet, "Apple died over an hour ago. She had two strong, healthy babies, but there was too much blood loss and internal bleeding. She didn't pull through." In a much lower voice, "I found Cale about five minutes ago. I'd come with some of Apple's friends to wish her and Cale well, and instead we found out she had...died."

"Oh Jesus."

"Nick, I think it's time for you to talk to him. Tell him I can help him with the children leaving if wants."

"Let me talk to him. But, Vesper don't go anywhere. O.K?"

Vesper handed Cale the cell.

"Hello Nick." Cale was trying to keep himself together, but he felt like crumbling.

"Hey, bro."

Cale couldn't speak. He took two deep breaths.

There was silence for a few seconds. Nick broke it.

Nick had tears going down his cheeks as he said, "Wish I was there Cale, because I have no idea what to say over the phone."

"I'm glad you called back." Cale said as he gulped air. "I'm fucked up right now."

"It sucks that it happened the way it did, Cale." Nick steadied his voice.

"I lied to her Nick. Me! I lied to her, straight to her face." Cale started to sob. He didn't care that Vesper was nearby. He was in pain and he couldn't control his emotions any longer. Between choking bursts he got out, "I told her she wasn't going to die, but I knew different." Cale cried harder. He had never cried like this in his life.

266

Nick said quietly, "Cale you made me proud to call you a friend a thousand times. Today, I'm most proud." Nick cleared his throat.

Cale kept crying, but he was a bit calmer.

"If Apple needed to hear she was O.K. from you, than that's what she needed to hear. You did the right thing. If you'd done it any other way it would have been wrong."

"I don't know about that, Nick."

"Cale you're supposed to be bummed out. Survivor's guilt is what you are feeling right now, bro. Don't just blame yourself that you're alive and she isn't."

Cale started to cry hard again.

"Hey Cale, cry." Nick felt more tears running down his cheeks. "Cry a lot. But remember, you are not alone now." Nick wiped his face. "You've got two babies and that's a lot of responsibility. Oh, and by the way, congratulations. I'll bet no one's even said that yet."

Cale took a long, halting breath and closed his eyes, "Thanks man. I'm really glad I get to talk to you right now, even if it's just over the phone."

"I know this is a tough time, but you need to focus. Right now, while Vesper is there, allow her to help you with the technicalities if you still want to get those tykes of yours out of Taiwan."

"I haven't even thought about that."

"Well first reality check as a father. You should get it sorted out. Now. My guess is it is time to leave Taiwan, as soon as you can. Vesper can help. Let her."

"I will." He wanted out of Taichung as quickly as possible. He guessed Apple's family would want to lay her to rest in Canada.

He already knew he wouldn't attend the funeral.

"O.K. Tough advice is coming. You need to try and be steely for the next couple days until the paper work is done."

"I get it. Thanks, Nick." Cale had stopped crying, but he let out a deep sigh.

"My phone will be on twenty-four-seven. You call any time you want. Anything you need, all you have to do is ask."

"I will."

"I love you, bro."

"Back at you, man." Cale wiped his eyes.

The line went dead. Cale looked at Vesper who was discreetly close.

"Nick said you could help." He gazed up to the black sky. The clouds covered the stars.

"Do you want to leave Taiwan?"

"Vesper, you've known me since day one in this country. Don't you think it's time I got out of here?" Cale mind had cleared fairly quickly. He was suddenly extremely lucid.

Vesper smiled. "Cale, there have been moments when I wished you had never come to Taiwan. This is not one of them. I am glad you're here." She put her hand under his chin and looked into his eyes. "Yes Cale, I think it is time for you to leave Taiwan." Then she pulled him into her body and hugged him tightly. He hugged her back.

Eventually, Vesper drove Cale home from the hospital. It took thirty minutes to get to his residence. They stayed silent the entire way. Vesper pulled into the parking lot and turned off the car.

Cale sat still in the seat looking straight ahead.

It was almost four in the morning.

"Cale, are you O.K.?" Vesper kept her voice quiet.

"I don't know if I'm ever going to be O.K." Cale's throat constricted.

"Cale, I would love to tell you everything is going to be fine. That your past means nothing." She paused trying to use the right English words. "Apple was a special person."

"I know." Cale whispered. He was barely able to keep his tears in check.

"I realize, you have lost many loved ones in your life." Vesper hesitated for a moment, "But you are such a strong person. You are very strong. And you will have to be. For them."

Cale looked over at her. He stayed silent, but tears started to well in his eyes.

"Cale, you have been given two gifts. You have a future starting."

"Not without Apple." Cale felt his heart breaking saying the words.

"You can't talk like that Cale. Apple would be sad you are hiding behind her death not to face what you have created."

"The babies?" Cale's voice was quiet and strained.

"No Cale. It's you that has been born. You came to Taiwan a man with no identity. Don't you remember?"

"Identity? I'm not following you Vesper." His voice stayed quiet.

"Cale what were you looking for when you came to Taiwan?"

Cale didn't know what to say. "I came because Helena wanted me to meet her grandmother."

"You tell the world that is why you came, but you were looking for something, we both know that. You now have what you came for, don't be blind."

"Vesper, you are talking in Chinese riddles and I'm not up for it. I'm beyond heartbroken and I don't need this psychoanalysis." Cale's voice was tired, and defensive.

"You're not the first or the last to have their heart broken. Healing, takes time. That is a fact."

"Is this some sort of salvation speech?" Cale said with bitterness. "I'm really lucky my wife died but I've got two kids…"

"What would you do if all three of them had died?"

Cale leaned back into the car seat. He looked out the window. It was starting to rain. He tried hard to imagine how he'd feel right now if the twins had been in the morgue along with Apple. He found himself remembering them asleep where he'd left them in the maternity ward.

"They are really cute aren't they?"

"Yes they are. And Cale, I will help you get them out of Taiwan." Vesper paused and brushed back her hair. "Your karma brought you to Taiwan, you know." Vesper sighed. "The result: two children who need a father." Softly, Vesper said, "You know what that is like, don't you?"

Cale nodded silently.

"Don't you want to give that to them?"

Cale nodded again. "Yes." His voice was quiet.

"Good, let's take the first step and start their lives properly. That's what Apple would have wanted you do right now." Vesper opened the car door and got out.

Cale got out and followed her into the apartment

building. When they got to the door he reached into his pocket to get his key. At the bottom of his pocket he came across the gift he'd intended to give Apple after the delivery. He pulled out the heart shaped locket.

Vesper looked at what he held in his hand.

"I was going to give it to her tonight. It was my mother's."

Vesper looked at his face. She could see the already puffy eyes beginning to shed more tears. "Well now you can give it to your daughter."

Cale looked at Vesper. "That's a good idea."

CHAPTER 23

New York
(Four months later)

The kids were still being great. Cale still found it difficult to believe that he had children. And twins. It was crazy.

"Are those tykes yours or did you kidnap them to prove you're really a father?"

Cale recognized Nick's voice immediately behind him. He turned around slowly.

"Oh, I'm sorry, are you nursing right now?" Nick smiled as he looked at the harness centered on Cale's chest.

Cale laughed. "Hey guys, Uncle Nick is here to bust your old man's balls."

Nick came close and looked closer at the two babies. "Jesus Cale, they really are beautiful. No bullshit." He looked up and smiled at his friend.

"Thanks."

"Thanks, nothing. Apple was their mother. They were destined to be cute." Nick looked back down at them both, nestled into their father's chest.

The baby girl, Peyton looked up at Nick. She smiled and slowly reached out her tiny hand.

Nick put his index finger close to her tiny palm. Peyton grasped it and gurgled. Tiny bubbles formed at her mouth.

Nick grinned and looked up to his friend who was watching intently, "You know Cale, life does hand out miracles sometimes."

The End

.